STUFFIE HOSPITAL: COLLECTION 1

ELLIE ROSE

Stuffie Hospital: Collection 1
Published by Claficionado Press Ltd
© 2023 Ellie Rose

All rights reserved.
This is a work of fiction. Names, characters, places, and incidents either are
the products of the author's imagination or are used fictitiously. Any
resemblance to actual persons, living or dead, businesses, companies, events,
or locales is entirely coincidental.

No part of this book may be reproduced or modified in any form, including
photocopying, recording, or by any information storage and retrieval system,
without express written permission from the author, except for the use of
brief quotations in a review.

Cover design © 2023 Ellie Rose

STUFFIE HOSPITAL ROMANCES

A Little's Unicorn (Lillie and Aiden's story)

A Little's Reindeer (Georgie and Warren's story)

A Little's Turtle (Bobbie and Marco's story)

A Little's Lion (Kacie and Dex's story)

A Little's Patchwork Bear (Ralphie and Nate's story)

A Little's Witchy Bear (Rylie and Eve's story)

A Little's Monster (Christie and Dana's story)

A Little's Dino (Archie and Rebecca's story)

A Little's Elephant (Frankie and Grey's story)

A Little's Owl (Darcie and Richard's story)

A Little's Pegasus (Beanie and Abigail's story)

CONTENT NOTES

A Little's Unicorn: Please be aware that this story contains references to a previous DDlg dynamic which was emotionally damaging for Lillie. The Dom is never seen on page, and his words and behaviours are challenged by Lillie and by other people when she speaks about him.

A Little's Reindeer: Please be aware that this story contains references to previous Daddy Doms who were mean to Georgie. They are never seen on page, and their words and behaviours are challenged by Warren when he hears about them. There is also a near car accident in the snow.

A Little's Turtle: Please be aware that this story contains references to a mean ex and the foster care system.

I hope that I have treated these experiences and emotions with the care that they and you deserve.

For my Queer Pack.
For my Little friends.
For this community.
Thank you for creating a space where I belong.

STUFFIE HOSPITAL

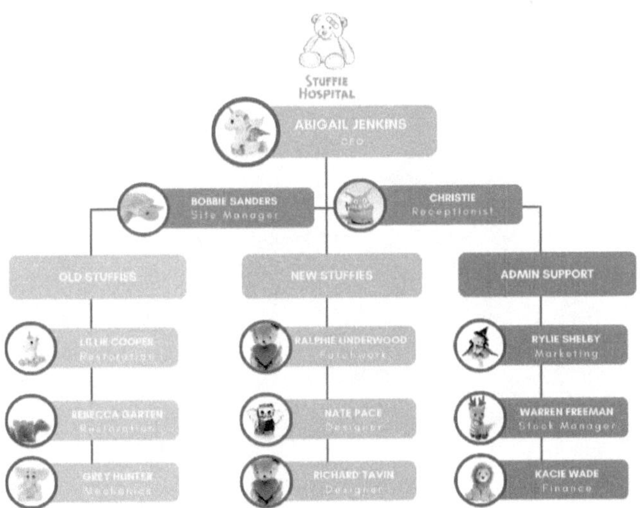

A LITTLE'S UNICORN

A
Little's
UNICORN

ELLIE ROSE

Lillie Cooper was up to her arms in soapy water, and she couldn't be happier.

"How's he looking, Lillie?" Rebecca, the other Restoration Specialist at Stuffie Hospital, looked over and grinned when she saw how much sudsy water had slopped over the side of the stuffie bath. "Wow, I swear, you end up cleaner than our patients do after a bath!"

Lillie giggled quietly, and nodded her head. It was true that she was probably a little enthusiastic when it came to cleaning the stuffies that came under her care, but she wanted to ensure that they felt refreshed as their owners would feel when they got to take them home again.

Pulling Daryl the Dino out, she set him down to dry on the side as she emptied the bath.

She hadn't quite been able to believe her luck when she'd landed this job. After leaving college, she'd really wanted to find something that used her degree in textiles, and her final project on restoring old fabrics had been the perfect example to use in her interview. Ms Owens had smiled approvingly when she'd waxed lyrical about different restoration techniques, and they'd offered her the job on the spot. It had felt so good to know that she was going to get to put her expertise to good use.

But more than that, she got to work with stuffies all day!

She gave Daryl a surreptitious pat on the head, and hid her smile. This really was the perfect job for a secret Little.

That weird, scrunchy feeling she got in her chest whenever she thought about the fact that her Little side was a secret flared up, and she rubbed her closed fist over her breastbone, getting suds all over the place.

It wasn't like it had always been a secret; she'd had a Daddy before, and spent time with him in Littlespace, and that had been really fun.

The scrunch intensified, and Lillie closed her eyes, trying to steady her breathing.

Because even if he'd never said it, she knew he hadn't thought that she was a very good Little. Why else would he have refused to read her stories? And told her that she was "too much" when she was all Littlespace excited and bubbly. That had really hurt. And it had hurt even more when he'd told her that he didn't love her, because he was supposed to be the one who looked after her and made sure that she didn't hurt. Instead, she'd found herself with tears rolling down her cheeks, barely recognising the stoic, shuttered man stood in front of her.

Yes. Much better to enjoy restoring stuffies at work, and push these feelings all the way down. Much easier to go on dates with beautiful women, handsome men and charming enbies, and never let on that she was dying to be praised and cuddled and cared for.

Her breathing evened out, but the scrunch didn't really go. It never seemed to dissipate completely these days, and the only thing that really helped was her job. And so, she threw herself wholeheartedly into her work.

Lillie noticed Rebecca looking at her worriedly, and smoothed her face over, taking Daryl over to the rinsing sink.

Everything was fine.

Besides, today was a big day for the business! Ms Owens had told them all in the staff meeting on Monday about the journalist who was coming to interview them for a national paper. They'd had quite a lot of press interest since a local news station had run a story about their work with the local children's hospital, and Lillie had to admit that the project was one of her favourite things to do. They got called in to the ward by the nurses whenever children had to have their hair cut, or before a particularly difficult surgery, and they'd give their teddy bears a shave, or carefully cut a stuffie open before sewing them shut again. It brought the children some level of comfort, to see their stuffies go through the same thing as them, and she was so glad that they'd started doing it.

She thought about the children's ward project, and her shoulders loosened a little. She was doing good in the little ways that she could, and that was enough for her.

The door to the Restoration Hub opened, and she heard Ms Owens walk in, talking to someone beside her. "And this is where we restore well-loved bears and other stuffies."

"It's a big room; I didn't realise the market for restoring toys was so large!" She didn't recognise the man's voice, but he sounded inquisitive, without the slightest trace of judgement, and there was a warmth that made Lillie look up from where she was rinsing Daryl.

The man was tall, with shoulder length dark hair that made her want to reach out and touch its shiny, silky strands. His broad shoulders cast a shadow over the sink as he came closer, and there was something about him that made her want that attention focused on her. But when she met his gaze, she almost flinched away from it. He was so direct in way that felt very *Daddy*, that she became very afraid that any kind of attention from him would be far too detrimental to her emotional wellbeing.

"Hi, I'm Aiden, Aiden Havers with the National Express. Do you mind if I ask you some questions?"

She shot a look at Ms Owens, who nodded at her kindly.

"Sure, what would you like to know?"

She expected questions about the project, and was a little taken aback when he pulled over a chair and perched on it, grinning up at her.

"I know all about the children's ward project; everyone knows that, I want to know about you."

"Me?" Lillie was fairly certain that she squeaked, and a traitorous blush rushed up, heating her cheeks.

"Exactly." Aiden's gaze was unwavering, but it wasn't unkind. Just steady. "I want to know about the people who work here at Stuffie Hospital, Nurse…?"

Fighting the urge to giggle, she answered him. "Lillie, although if we're being technical about it, I'm nurse, doctor and surgeon, all rolled into one."

"Is that so?"

She flickered her eyes to his, and his gentle, encouraging smile made her laugh, the sound echoing round the hub, and causing Rebecca and Grey from Mechanics to look over at them curiously. "Exactly so. Would you like the tour?"

"I'd like nothing better." When he stood up, she realised that she was going to have to crane her neck to look up at him. That was the problem with being short, everyone always hovered above you.

There was a split second where her mind conjured up the image of Aiden Havers shirtless above her, looking down at her with that same intense focus, before she blushed furiously again.

"Where would you like to start, Doctor Lillie?"

Lillie almost reached out her hand to grab his, before she remembered herself and stopped just in time. There was a pause and she closed her eyes, praying that he hadn't noticed. It wasn't her fault; he made her feel Big and Little all at once, so that she was completely confused.

"Lillie?" His voice was closer and when she opened her eyes, she realised that he'd leaned in slightly to see if she was okay, his hair brushing softly against her cheek.

"I'm sorry." The words blurted out in a bit of a rush and even as she heard herself speak, she tried to pull them back, stem the flow of the tide. "I didn't mean to- I wouldn't have- I'm just *so* embarrassed. It's best to start the tour over there, and I forgot for a moment that you don't work here and-"

"It's okay." His words cut through the babbling brook of her voice, and she stopped. Breathed. Waited for the scrunch to kick in and remind her to keep her Little firmly reined in. Waited for him to make an awkward joke that hid how too much he thought she really was. "I think it's lovely that you're so enthusiastic about your job. And I'm sorry for teasing you; I didn't mean to make you flustered."

He seemed genuine.

And he was looking at her cautiously, as if she were a skittish horse who'd rear up and run at the slightest provocation.

She checked for the scrunch.

No scrunch.

"I don't mind the teasing. I'm just not used to it, is all."

He nodded sagely, and she wanted to bury her face in his chest and have him stroke her hair until she knew–truly knew, deep down in her soul–that he wasn't just saying that it was okay. "That seems fair. How about I dial it back a bit for the tour then?"

Lillie nodded. "Yes please."

She still felt his eyes on her throughout the tour though, even if he wasn't teasing her, and he listened to her–genuinely listened–as she talked about treating particularly delicate fabrics, and the differences between all the different kinds of brushes on the brush station. He even asked questions about the process, and she liked that he was interested, even if it was just for the article.

And finally, they came to what Ralphie, who did patchwork, called 'The Great Wall of Stuffies'. It was made up of the oldest, tattiest stuffies you could possibly imagine. Some, where their stitching barely bound joints to body, or where they'd been so well loved that they were patchy all over.

"Well, they all just look so sad," Aiden commented, and Lillie rounded on him furiously.

"No they don't, they're just waiting patiently."

He didn't call her out on answering him back, but she felt an undercurrent of *something* as he looked at her.

"It's mean to say that they look sad; and I don't like to think that they're sad because then it would be too hard to walk past them every day."

He nodded as if to say that he understood. "So, they're waiting patiently?"

"Exactly." She walked over to the wall and looked up at it, taking in all the worn faces. "They've all had such happy lives, and they're waiting for us to repair them so they can go out and make more people happy."

"Oh, so they're not clients?"

"Kind of," she paused, gathering her thoughts together, and trying to place her firmly in Bigspace. It didn't really work; the Great Wall of Stuffies always called to her Little.

"These are the stuffies who have been given to us by people who don't need them anymore. And when we're a bit quieter, or our current project is having to wait before the next stage," she gestured over to where Daryl the Dino was drying out, "then we work on restoring one of these."

"And what happens to them after that?" Aiden's voice made Lillie feel a little bit wobbly, like he knew where all her weak spots were, and his words were poking at them. A gentle poke, and a poke that was probably long overdue, but one that made her want to cry a bit, nonetheless.

"After that we give them away. To the children's ward, if there are new patients who don't have stuffies of their own; to the local DV shelter; sometimes, one of the team falls in love with one and asks to take them home. They get homes, it just sometimes takes a little time."

"Which ones have you taken home?" he asked, and she felt herself shrink.

"I don't have any stuffies."

As soon as she spoke, Lillie wished she could pick up the words and hoover them back into her mouth. She hadn't intended on answering him; why couldn't she have just lied and said that she'd picked up a rabbit or something? But that something in his voice that made her feel wobbly, also made her realise that she couldn't lie to him. That she didn't *want* to lie to him.

Aiden was silent, and when she peeked at him, he looked sad.

"It's okay, really." But it wasn't, and the brightness in her voice was brittle. "There are so many children who deserve a stuffie far more than I do."

He took a step towards her, and she was surprised to notice a look of determination on his face. "Lillie, *everyone* deserves stuffies. Even stuffie doctors who spend their time repairing bears for everyone else."

Oh. Her mouth fell open, and then she almost did cry.

He thought she should have a stuffie.

"Really, it's…"

"No." Now that look of determination was rock solid, and it did not budge. "It's not okay. You deserve a stuffie. I will find you a stuffie."

❧　2　☙

There were other Littles at Stuffie Hospital; Ralphie, who did patchwork, had pretty much enveloped her in hugs from their first day, and though he'd never said he thought Lillie was a Little, he'd encouraged her to carry the patients she was working on around with her during the day. Which was the only reason why Daryl the Dino was currently tucked under her arm, and certainly didn't have anything to do with the fact that she was still a little stunned by Aiden's determination to find her a stuffie of her own.

"Lillie! Over here!" Ralphie waved at her enthusiastically as she walked into the staff room, as if there was anywhere else that he could have been, and pulled out a chair.

"Hey Ralphie."

"I heard that you met the reporter?"

She nodded, suddenly even more tongue tied than usual.

"What's he like?"

"He…he…"

Ralphie stopped mid-bite and put his sandwich down. "Lillie Cooper, what aren't you telling me?"

All of a sudden, she couldn't hold it back any longer,

words coming bubbling up in a wave of excitement that she'd long ago learnt to hide. "Ralphie, he was so nice and so interested in *everything* and I showed him all round the workshop, and my stations, and the Great Wall of Stuffies and then…and then…"

She found herself stuttering, as if her words were so desperate to escape that they were tripping over themselves in order to do so. "And then he said he wants to find *me* a stuffie!"

Ralphie blinked a couple of times, "So?"

"So, I don't have any stuffies."

There was a moment of silence in which Ralphie took a long sip from the juice box in his packed lunch, before setting it down and looking at her directly. "Do you mean to tell me that you don't have any stuffies? *You.* Queen of the restoration station."

Lillie looked back down at her lunch and took a bite of her sandwich. "And?"

"But you're a…" he paused, and shot a look at where Daryl the Dino was sat on the chair next to her. "I mean, I always just assumed that you were…like me."

"Like you?" Lillie knew exactly what he meant, but that scrunchie feeling was back and she wanted to push up from her chair and go back to work rather than talk about it, but this was *Ralphie*. Ralphie who was always the first with hugs in the morning, and who encouraged her to talk more, and made her laugh.

Ralphie was her friend. Ralphie was safe.

He looked confused now, his face slightly scrunched up as if trying to work out what to say next.

"I am. Like you, that is." Today was a day for blurting things out it appeared, and Lillie very steadfastly did not look at her friend. No big deal. Just sharing her biggest secret with someone from her job. Totally fine. No reason to panic.

A hand slipped into hers. "That's okay. It's *better* than okay. Lillie, we can have so much fun!"

She must have looked more than a little terrified, because Ralphie dialled it right back and lowered his voice to a calm, resolute tone that sounded nothing like his normal self.

"Look, there's an event I go to once a week, which is running tonight. A social event for people like us, and people who like to look after us."

"Like a munch?"

"Exactly that! It's a munch for Littles and caregivers."

Lillie thought hard. She'd been to munches before, meetups for kinksters who just wanted to hang out and chat, without the pressure of having to talk about their kinky interests, but also without the need to hide it either. But those had all been grown up munches, that she'd gone with her previous Daddy. She'd never been to one on her own, and certainly never been to one for Littles.

Ralphie squeezed her hand. "You're a solo Little, right?"

She looked at him, a bit confused. "Solo Little?"

"A Little who doesn't have a caregiver. I'm a solo Little too!" For a moment, his smile dimmed. "It can be hard sometimes, but it doesn't mean that I don't get to be Little, and having other Little friends makes that a lot easier. I promise."

AND THAT WAS HOW, some hours after work, Lillie found herself with half her wardrobe strewn over her bed, almost in the middle of a meltdown. Ralphie was supposed to be picking her up to go the munch in fifteen minutes, and she still had no idea what to wear.

It was all very confusing. She had Little clothes, that was true, but she wasn't sure if they were *too* Little, or if it would be inappropriate to wear them to a pub. Her fingers flitted over the edge of her favourite Little dress. It was pink, with pretty ruffles, and a white bow right below the neckline. After her breakup, it had been the one Little thing she'd allowed herself to buy, just for her, but she'd never worn it. For weeks, it had been hanging on the outside of her wardrobe, and she looked at it each night when she went to bed, wondering whether the next day would be the day she'd try it on.

Taking a deep breath, she grabbed the dress and pulled it on over her head, allowing herself a little twirl as it settled about her knees.

It was pretty! *She* was pretty.

Somehow, that simple decision loosed her Little side and before she knew it, she'd pulled on knee-high pink fluffy socks, a headband, and her chunky Mary Jane shoes.

Spinning around, she caught a glimpse of herself in the mirror and she giggled, the sound burst forth like a sun after the rain. The scrunch that had been threatening to overwhelm her chest dissipated and she breathed in long and deep, for what felt like the first time in months.

Lillie hadn't quite realised what an impact wearing her Little clothes would have. It was like they'd taken her right there to that joyful place, where she was never too much, and where nothing could ever hurt her.

There was a sharp rap at her apartment door, and she flew across the room to open it, beaming when Ralphie stood there. He looked adorable, in a cute button-up shirt and shorts with dinosaurs on them, and his mouth dropped open when he looked at her. "Lillie! You look so *Little*! He took her hand and spun her on the spot, and as she came to a stop, she clapped her hands in delight, her skirt flowing round her.

"It's not too Little?"

He helped her on with her coat and grinned. "Not at all! We have a private room booked, so we don't disturb any vanillas by accident." He paused for a moment. "I'm going to have to Big whilst I drive, but when we get there, we can be Little together?"

She nodded enthusiastically. "I'd love that!"

"Oh, and I think someone else from work might be there; Kacie? From Finance? Is that okay?"

Suddenly, Lillie realised that it really was okay. She was fine with someone else from Stuffie Hospital knowing, and besides, if Kacie was there, then it meant that she understood.

As she belted herself up in Ralphie's car, she had a small moment of scrunch. There was a reason she hadn't gone to munches on her own before; big groups of people were sometimes far too overwhelming for her, but as if he knew how she was feeling, Ralphie reached over and squeezed her hand.

"It's going to be great Lillie. And if you need a break, just tell me."

They chatted during the car ride, talking about work and the various stuffies they'd been working on, before pulling up in a car park behind the pub where the munch was being held. It wasn't too far from Lillie's apartment and she marvelled at the fact that there'd been a whole Little community right under her nose, if only she'd thought to look for it.

Stopping off to grab sodas at the bar, they linked hands before heading up the stairs to the private room.

The wall of sound that hit her when she entered made her stumble for a moment, but Ralphie was right there as she righted herself, holding her glass and giving her a moment to adjust.

The room was bustling full of people; some standing and talking, whilst others were clustered around tables. Ralphie tugged on her hand and drew her towards the back of the room, where cushions and blankets had been arranged on the floor, and where a trio of people were sat.

"Lillie, meet Archie, Frankie, and you know Kacie already."

She waved at them shyly, holding onto the comforting softness of her dress with her other hand. They all smiled up at her and Kacie shifted over to make space for them both.

"Come sit with us, Lillie."

Lillie fought the urge to circle on the spot before sitting down, but gave in and let out a sigh of relief when she plonked her bum onto a very soft pillow. "Hi everyone."

"It's Lillie's first time," said Ralphie, throwing himself down to lie next to them. "So we gotta be extra nice to her!"

Kacie and Archie grabbed an array of colouring pencils and piled them all into her lap, gabbling at a hundred miles an hour, and she must have looked a little overwhelmed because Frankie quietly shuffled a little closer and offered up their elephant stuffie for her to meet. That was good, she could do stuffies. Taking his leg, she shook it seriously, and then let a little giggle escape.

Before she knew it, she had been corralled into helping them all colour in a huge picture of a mermaid that they'd spread out on the floor, and sat smiling to herself quietly as they all talked around her.

Archie and Kacie were as talkative as Ralphie, but she felt especially comfortable with Frankie, the Little enby being quiet, just like Lillie herself.

"We're all solo Littles," Ralphie explained as they coloured, "so we have to look out for each other. And being Little with other Littles is far more fun than being Little on your own." As if to prove their point, he tackled Kacie with tickles so that he could sneak the orange pencil away from her. Their laughter was infectious, and Lillie couldn't help but laugh along with them.

Soon though, she was thirsty again, and clambered up, asking if anyone else wanted something to drink. They were all okay, and so she headed down the stairs herself, half skipping as she reached the bottom.

Waiting to be served, she hummed to herself by the bar, shifting from foot to foot in time with the overhead music, completely lost in her happy space. In fact, it wasn't until a deep voice exclaimed, "Doctor Lillie?" that she realised that the bar staff had been trying to get her attention.

She ordered some water and then turned to see Aiden standing behind her.

He still wore the same suit from earlier, but he'd undone his top button, and rolled up his sleeves so that she got a glimpse of muscled forearms that looked like they belonged to a fireman, rather than a writer.

"Aiden!" Tugging at her skirt, she went red, and then even redder, when she suddenly remembered how she was dressed. Properly Little. "What are you…I mean…why…I…"

"I'm here for the meetup, upstairs," he said, taking pity on her before she got much more flustered. "How about yourself?"

"Oh, I'm here for that too. My friend brought me tonight."

"Your friend?"

She realised what he was asking, "Oh no, nothing like that; he just thought-" and then, to her embarrassment, she got stuck on the word thought, and started repeating it over and over, in an attempt to jump start her mouth into finishing the sentence. "…thought…thought… thought…*thought* that I would like it. Because I'm, well."

Aiden didn't interrupt her stammering, just waited patiently with that deliciously calm smile on his face, until she was able to get all of her words out again. "He seems like a good friend."

"Ralphie's the best! He's introduced me to people and I've

actually made some other Little friends and it's been so much fun!" Lillie beamed up at Aiden, and then blinked rapidly, realising quite how effusive she'd been; wanting to backtrack immediately.

"Making Little friends seems like an excellent use of your time. I'm not a Little, but would you mind if I spent some time talking to you this evening too?"

"You're not a Little? Then why are you...ohhhhhhhhh." She answered her own question and blushed, "You're a caregiver?"

He nodded, "That I am. I'm a Daddy Dom."

The moment he said the word Daddy, Lillie felt herself melt a tiny bit. There was something so right about that word being applied to him, that she ducked her head and took a sip of water.

"And how about yourself, Doctor Lillie?"

The pet name made her shyness melt away, and she found herself rolling her eyes at him. "Like you don't know." And she got a thrill when he raised his eyebrows at her. Oh. Was this how bratting could feel? She'd never much enjoyed being naughty—it always triggered her anxiety—but this felt impish rather than naughty, and rather like he was in on the joke too.

"That kind of response could only come from a Little. And a bratty one at that."

But the word bratty set off a scrunch in her chest, no matter how teasingly he'd said it, and he must have recognised it in her face because he stopped teasing, his face serious. "Lillie?"

"Maybe not bratty? Maybe just mischievous?"

Aiden smiled. "I like mischievous. It's a nice way to describe that kind of behaviour. Now, Doctor Lillie, might I take your water for you, as we go up the stairs?"

She liked that he'd asked, not just assumed, and handed her drink to him with a shy smile. "Thank you."

"Thank *you*. Now, after you." And as she scampered up the stairs, the sound of his heavy tread behind her made her feel very Little indeed.

When Aiden gave Lillie her glass of water back, she hovered for a moment, unsure of what to do next, rocking back and forth on the spot.

"Why don't you show me where you've been sitting with your friends?"

"I can do that!" She reached out for his hand, not faltering, like she had done at work, and he took her hand in his. His hand was big and warm, and practically engulfed hers. It felt nice. Better than nice, it felt safe. And Lillie pulled him over to the blanket corner, and showed him the picture that they'd all been working on.

"Wow, that's some excellent colouring in." His words were addressed to all five of them, but Aiden was looking at Lillie as he said it, and she flushed with pleasure.

There was a chorus of "Hi Aiden"s, and she realised that he must be a regular at the munch.

Ralphie shot her a look and grinned. "How did you meet Aiden?"

She stumbled over her words, not knowing whether she should out him as having met him at work or…

"I was interviewing Lillie here at her work today, and then we bumped into each other downstairs at the bar."

Ralphie nodded before dropped his pencil, clearly suddenly realising that Aiden had been the reporter at Stuffie Hospital earlier that afternoon, who'd been so determined to find Lillie a stuffie. "Lillie is really lovely," he said, his Little voice slipping away for a moment.

Lillie looked between them, slightly confused as Aiden and Ralphie eyed each other.

"Yes, she is, and I'm hoping to get to know her some more." Aiden's voice was level, but she couldn't tell what he was thinking. This was getting a smidgeon awkward. She adored Ralphie, but Lillie really *really* hated confrontation, and if the two of them…

"Okay!" Ralphie's voice was back to being singsong, and when she looked at him, he nodded at her encouragingly. "Lillie, why don't you sit next to Aiden on that blanket over there? Maybe do some colouring together?"

Now that was a lovely idea. "Would you like to do some colouring in with me?" She tried not to show how she held her breath, hoping beyond hope that this lovely man, who seemed so kind and interested in her, would want to do such a thing.

"I'd love that Doctor Lillie." His smile was genuine, and she clambered on her knees over to where the pile of colouring books were, flicking through them until she found the perfect picture for them to do together, and then clambering back to where he sat on the blankets.

"Unicorns?"

"I like unicorns." Her shyness was melting away now, especially as he was sat, all cross-legged on the blankets. It was such a contrast, the grey suit dark against the pastels of the cushions, and she giggled. "They're magical and they get to be all kinds of rainbow colours."

"Rainbow colours are excellent." His voice was serious, but there was a twinkle in his eye that let her know that he wasn't teasing her too much. He picked up a green pencil and started colouring the unicorn's mane. "So, why don't you tell me about yourself?"

She picked out a sky-blue colour and started doing the tail. "I already did that, at work today."

"Yes, but that was work you. What does outside of work you do?"

"You mean Little me?"

"If you're comfortable with that."

Lillie thought hard, and coloured in just as hard as she tried to work out what to say. "Well, I like being happy, an' I like colouring in, an' I like unicorns."

"All of those things seem like very good things. Do you get to do that very often?"

She stopped colouring.

"I haven't done it in a long time."

He didn't push her to continue, just kept colouring, his dark head bent, intent on the unicorn in front of him.

"I had a Daddy a long time ago and when he left," she paused, waiting for the inevitable scrunch to subside before continuing, "I forgot how to be Little."

Aiden stopped colouring for a moment. "Those seem like pretty Big feelings Lillie. We can talk about something else if you'd like."

She shook her head and continued colouring. "I's okay. I have the stuffies I work with, an' they're *adorable*, an' I have Ralphie."

"But no stuffies of your own."

"No, but I have books!"

"Books?"

"Yes, I have lots and lots and lots of Little books. I read

them to myself, of course, but maybe one day I'll have someone who wouldn't mind reading them to me."

"I can't imagine anyone who'd mind reading you books, little one."

Her eyes must have been the size of plates, because he dropped his pencil. "I'm sorry Lillie, I should have asked first before calling you that. That wasn't okay."

"I...I kind of liked it." Her voice was so quiet he had to lean in to hear her. "If you don't mind?"

"I definitely don't mind." And then he picked up his pencil and carried on colouring in.

"Aiden...?"

"Yes, little one?"

"Do you have a Little of your own?"

His sigh was sad, and it made her want to curl up in his lap and give him all the cuddles in the world, until he stopped sighing like that. "No Lillie, I don't have my own Little. Like you, it's been quite some time."

She slipped her hand into his and squeezed. "It's a bit lonely sometimes, isn't it?"

"Yes, it is, little one, but that's okay. I'm happy to wait until I find the Little who wants to be mine."

And they carried on colouring in like that, hand in hand, silently painting the unicorn in all of the colours of the rainbow. Silence usually made Lillie feel uncomfortable in a different way to noise. Noise was overwhelming and made you want to hide under a blanket, but silence... Silence was the sound of disapproval, of a rule having been broken that she didn't know existed. Or at least, that's how it had always felt to her before. This time was different though. This time it felt like the split second on a beach after a wave crashes against the shore, just before it shucks pebbles as it crawls back to the sea. Like waiting for something to begin.

Her hair fell across the page as she leant forward, and Aiden leaned and tucked it back behind her ear.

"Thank you, Aiden," she said. "I don't want to colour in my hair by accident!"

"No, little one, we certainly wouldn't want that to happen."

It was a small oasis in the midst of the munch. Lillie was vaguely aware of other Littles coming to sit on the blankets, and colour in the giant mermaid, or just sit with their stuffies and chat, but she was very comfortable in her bubble with Aiden.

"I like you," she said impetuously, Little space shouting down the Big voice that told her that normal people didn't say such things.

"I like you too Lillie. And," he paused here and chucked her under her chin until she was looking up at him, "if it's okay, I'd like to get to know you better. Your Little makes me feel all kinds of protective around you, but I'd like to get to know Big you as well. Maybe we could go for dinner at some point this week?"

She nodded eagerly, unable to keep the grin from spreading all across her face. "Yes, I'd like that. Very much."

"Okay then," Aiden's voice was suddenly more confident, and she realised suddenly that he must have been nervous, asking her out. "Is there any food you don't like? Any food that you particularly do?"

"I love Italian food," she said, "pasta is super yummy. But filled pasta is the absolute bestest!"

"I think I can find somewhere that does filled pasta for you."

Lillie clapped her hands in excitement, and Ralphie shuffled over to them. "Excited clapping? Yay! I like a happy Lillie!" She didn't miss the searching look he gave Aiden, but as he dropped it much quicker than he had earlier, she didn't say anything. "Lillie lovely, I'm going to have to get Big fairly soon, because it's nearly closing time."

She looked at her phone, and sure enough, it was nearly 11. "Can I take your number please? So that we can message about dinner?"

"Of course, we can," Aiden said, and typed it in for her. "Would you also mind texting me when you get home?"

"Oh it's okay, Ralphie's driving me."

"I know, but I'd like to know that you're all home safe and sound anyway. You bring out the protective side in me little one."

Lillie found herself going all shy again. It was one thing to call her little one when it was just the two of them, but in front of Ralphie? But when she looked up, Ralphie was smiling encouragingly. "Okay, I can do that."

"Good girl. Shall I help you get your coat?"

As he helped her on with her coat, she whispered, "Aiden?"

He leaned in close to hear her. "Yes, little one?"

"Ummmm...I kind of want to call you Daddy when I'm Little. Is that wrong?"

The warmth in his eyes flooded her until she felt warm all over. "It's definitely not wrong, little one, but I think we should have a talk about it when you're Big, so that you're not making decisions in Little space that you'd regret later."

The scrunch hit her hard, and she almost drew back from him, but he caught up her face in his hands. "Now now, little one, none of that. I'm not saying no at all. But it wouldn't be very responsible and Daddy-like of me to say yes whilst you're all floaty and Little now, would it?"

"I suppose not." Her words sounded cautious, but the scrunch subsided somewhat, and she was able to breathe normally.

"Are you free tomorrow? Because I really would like to talk to you about that, and get to know you better."

She thought and then nodded.

"Excellent, I will message you about all of the details," and then all of a sudden, his lips were pressing against her forehead and it was almost as if she'd forgotten how to breathe. "I leave you in Ralphie's safe hands, little one. And do remember to text me when you get home."

"I will," she breathed, and then her arm was linked with Ralphie's and she was being bustled off down the stairs.

THE CAR RIDE home was far from quiet. Ralphie bombarded her with question after question, and it was only when he paused for breath that she was able to get a word in edgeways.

"Why did you go all Big when you were talking to Aiden, Ralphie?"

Ralphie glanced over at her. "So, our Littles are pretty vulnerable, right? And today was the first time you've ever acknowledged to me that you're a Little. Aiden is nice, and he's not the kind of Daddy Dom who goes home after the munch with a different Little each week, in fact, I'm not sure I've ever seen him take a Little home, but you're *you*, Lillie. You're sweet, and quiet, and shy, and someone needs to look out for you. I'm really excited for you, but I also want to make sure you don't get hurt either, because I don't like it when my friends get hurt."

"We're *friends* friends, Ralphie?"

He looked confused at her question. "Of course we are; I wouldn't invite just anyone to a munch. We started off as work friends, but we most definitely are friends friends Lillie."

That was good to know. Making new friends was always

a little difficult, because she never quite understood all the unspoken rules that everyone had around friendships, so she could never quite work out where that left her.

And she'd definitely *thought* they were proper friends, but she didn't like to assume, so the confirmation was definitely welcome.

"You're really sweet, looking out for me. I appreciate it. I don't want to get hurt again, because my last experience with a Daddy was…" her voice trailed off. She didn't quite know how to encapsulate in words how it had felt to realise that he just didn't want her because she, and all of her idiosyncrasies, were too much for him to bear.

She realised that she was jiggling her leg up and down, and forced herself to stop before it annoyed Ralphie. Wait. That wasn't fair. She wasn't giving him a chance. "Do you mind if I jiggle my leg?"

"Why would I mind? Stim away, lovely."

So, she did, running her fingers up and down her arms, and moving her legs in time to the music on the radio. It was a comfort and a relief to just react in the moment. "I really like him, I think."

"I can tell, and he is really nice. How about when you go on this dinner, you message me when he picks you up, when you get to the restaurant, and when you get home? No matter how nice someone is, it's good to be safe."

"I can do that, but we may just meet at the restaurant."

Ralphie laughed, "From how he was looking at you, sweetness, I'm pretty certain he's going to spoil you rotten. I'm not sure you're going to need to walk anywhere ever again, with Daddy Aiden on the scene."

※ 4 ※

As soon as Lillie's key hit the lock, she had to fight to stop herself from running straight through to her bedroom, and getting under the covers so that she could get all cosy and message Aiden. No, she had things to do first, but she sent off a quick message before she tidied up.

LILLIE: Hi there Aiden! Lillie here. Home safe and sound.

HE REPLIED ALMOST INSTANTLY.

AIDEN: Thank you for letting me know, little one. It's quite late; are you going straight to bed?

Lillie: I have to tidy up a bit first, and sort myself beforehand, but then I'm going to get all cosy.

Aiden: Well, aren't you a good girl? Why don't you drop me a message once you're tucked up, and we'll talk a bit about dinner tomorrow?

Lillie: Okay!! :)

LILLIE WASN'T sure that she'd ever gotten ready for bed as fast she did then. A whizz around the apartment, picking up her clothes from where they were strewn across her bed, then straight to her bathroom to take off her makeup and brush her teeth. Clothes thrown into her laundry basket before she pulled on soft pink pyjamas and jumped onto her bed, pulling the covers up around her.

She took a breath.

Snuggled under her duvet.

And then turned back to her phone.

LILLIE: All done!

Aiden: Well done you, that was quick!

Lillie: Thank you. :) I didn't have too much to do.

Aiden: Are you nice and cosy now?

Lillie: Yes, thank you.

Aiden: You have such pretty manners, little one, all ps and qs. Very sweet, but I need you to be Big for me for a minute. Is that okay?

SHE POPPED her phone onto her pillow for a moment and closed her eyes. Breathed in and then breathed out. Once, twice, three times until she felt completely relaxed. And when she opened her eyes, the chaotic excitement of her Little had faded into the background, and she was Big again.

LILLIE: Of course, it is. I'm big now Aiden.

Aiden: Great. So, would you be comfortable with me picking you up from home, or would you rather I pick you up from somewhere public?

THAT HADN'T BEEN something she'd really considered, despite Ralphie's assertions that Aiden would want to pick her up. It was quite a big deal, him knowing where she lived, and she wasn't sure how she felt about that.

LILLIE: Well, my apartment building should be fine, but perhaps I could come down and meet you at the front desk?

Aiden: That seems like an excellent idea, and that way I can drop you home after, so you don't have to travel back in the dark. Good plan!

Lillie: Ralphie also said that I should set up some check ins with him as well.

Aiden: Ralphie is very sensible; your safety always comes first with me, Lillie. Why don't you also give him my number, so he can call if he gets worried?

Lillie: Okay! What time would you like to pick me up?

Aiden: How about 7? That way you've enough time to get home after work, and we've plenty of time to hang out together.

Lillie: That sounds great, thank you. I'm looking forward to it.

Aiden: So am I Lillie, more than you know.

AFTER THEY'D WISHED each other good night, Lillie put her phone down and tried to sleep, but every time she closed her eyes, all she could see was his face, close to hers.

There was certainly nothing at all Little about how she felt when she thought of the intensity in his eyes. She was all Big, with Big wants and Big desires. And right now, what she wanted most of all was to think of the way his hand had felt on hers. It'd been big, and strong, and she imagined it now, covering hers, and pulling her hand down below the covers.

Lillie let her right hand slip beneath the waistband of her pyjama bottoms and drift down between her legs, just as her left snuck up to tweak her aching nipples. She was wet already, and when she ran a finger up through her lips to her clit, she could feel the ghost of his lips upon her forehead.

She wanted those lips everywhere.

Trailing kisses down her neck, puckered around each tight nipple, and pressed up against her pussy, ready to lap at the nectar she produced. She wanted him, to fill her pussy with his fingers, his tongue, and to make her come apart for him, over and over.

Her fingers danced across her clit, thrumming it just how she liked, and Lillie's eyes stayed tightly closed, his face dancing behind her eyelids. How would he look at her now? Would he watch and then tell her she was a good girl in that deep voice of his, as she came for him? Her breath hitched and her hips arched up off the bed, involuntarily responding to the words that she heard echoing in her mind. *Good girl, good girl.* She wanted to be a good girl. She wanted to be *his* good girl, and…

Lillie cried out as her pussy spasmed beneath her fingers, that fluttering feeling in her clit washing over her until she slumped back on her bed. Spent.

Had she really just orgasmed whilst fantasising about a man she'd only met that day? Part of her wanted to blush, to deny it, but another part revelled in the fact that she'd taken her own pleasure; done something for herself, whilst thinking of a man who clearly liked her.

Curling up, she nestled under the covers, and drifted off into a land of dreams where Aiden's lips whispered good girl everywhere she turned.

· · ·

THE NEXT DAY AT WORK, Lillie was all over the place.

She dropped Daryl the Dino so many times that she felt like he needed an apology all his own; kept zoning out, and having to shake her head to bring herself back into the room; and then tripped over nothing at all and cut her knee when running to the stock cupboard.

Warren Freeman, Stuffie Hospital's stock manager, made her sit down and handed her some band-aids. "You've been running around a lot today Lillie, is everything okay?"

Was everything okay? She'd woken to a text from Aiden —*Good morning lovely girl*—and had walked around in a haze for the first half hour of her day, almost making her late for work. But that hadn't been a bad haze.

"I'm okay, I'm just a little distracted." She smiled to herself and Warren laughed.

"Ah, I see, that kind of distracted. Well, try not to run so much in the workshops, because you don't want to hurt yourself again."

She nodded and got up to head back over to her station, where Daryl was waiting for her. Time for brushes.

Brushing out the dinosaur stuffie's fur was actually a really good call. It allowed her to sit and decompress after a morning of zooming around. She'd been hyperfocusing so hard on the date later that evening, that everything else had kind of gone by in a blur. But now she got to stop and breathe, and focus on nothing but the swish swish swish of the brush across the stuffie's fur.

Being a Little was fun in many ways, but she'd forgotten how her overexcitement could tire her out very quickly.

Swish swish swish.

This was one of her favourite parts of the restoration. She knew that it was only aesthetics, that the replacing of the stuffing, and the heart that Ms Owens herself crafted and placed inside each stuffie, was far more important, but it made her feel like she was looking after them properly. Caring for them, just like their owners would when they got to go home.

She paused for a moment and looked across to the Great Wall of Stuffies. Why had she never taken a stuffie home? There were more than enough of them, and no one at Stuffie Hospital would have minded; in fact, they often came down to pick out a lucky toy to be taken home to be loved. But for some reason, she'd never done so.

Why did it only feel safe to love other people's stuffies?

Lillie looked down at where Daryl was sat on her desk, brushed fur shining. She'd spent a whole week looking after this dinosaur, even carrying it around with her during her day, and yet…

She shrugged and picked up the brush again, but this time her swishes felt somewhat deflated, and she might have even let a tear fall, if her phone hadn't dinged.

AIDEN: Hey there little one, I hope you're having a good day!

MAYBE IT WAS THE DISTRACTION, or maybe it was just the delight she felt because he'd thought of her, but her swishes picked up some more, and soon she was back in the brushing zone.

After work, Ralphie came home with her, to help her pick out an outfit.

"It's a Big date, so I want to look cute *and* hot," she said.

"Cute and hot? Oh darling, you can totally pull that off." Ralphie was like a tornado in her wardrobe, pulling and discarding clothes until her bedroom was a litany of fabrics strewn everywhere.

Being a textiles girl, Lillie didn't really have much black in her wardrobe. It looked great on people, and she knew that a little black dress should be a staple in any femme wardrobe, but she lived for patterns and colours. Weirdly enough, it was whole blocks of colour that she found more overwhelming, which was why even in her pink outfits, there were different shades of pink sat together.

There was a shout of delight, and then Ralphie pulled out a dress that Lillie had forgotten she even had. It was a belted halter neck dress, with a ruffled skirt that flounced out and a hemline that flirted around the knees. She remembered when she saw the pattern for the first time, peeking out from a pile in a fabric shop window, and she hadn't been able to resist running in and buying some on the spot. One of her friends on the fashion course had made it for her, and she'd modelled in it as part of their final project runway.

Lillie wasn't usually a floral pattern kind of person, but this didn't have flowers on it. Just leaves. Thousands of tiny leaves, in every colour imaginable, overlaying a black background, on a fabric that made her skin sing.

She took the hanger and was flooded with warmth, her pulse rocketing as she thought of how she'd look in it.

"This one."

"Like I'd let you choose anything else!"

All dressed up, she piled her hair up on her head, dark curls escaping defiantly from where she pinned them in place, and twirled in front of the mirror. The skirt spun satisfyingly. And she paused for a moment. This was a Big dress, and she'd picked out pretty heels to go with it, but maybe…

Yes. She needed the full underwear armour feeling— wearing lacy battle gear beneath her clothes, to help her stand taller, and give her more confidence. And that meant getting out her suspender belt. Pulling on each stocking felt like a ritual in itself, just like the process of getting ready to go out, and by the time she was done, she felt like she could take on anything.

Lillie couldn't remember the last time when waiting felt less like a scrunch and more like butterflies. Her hands flitted between fluttering by her sides, and fiddling with the hem of her skirt, slipping in and out of the inbuilt pockets. She'd sipped water about four or five times, and almost worn a hole in her carpet, pacing back and forth. Ralphie had given her a hug and reminded her to check in before he left, and so now it was just her. Waiting.

Her phone buzzed, and she glanced at it before grabbing her bag and her keys, and heading out her door.

As she headed down the stairs, towards the lobby, she couldn't stop herself from the occasional happy skip or jump. It had been a long time since she'd been on a date with someone who knew about her Little side. It might be a Big date, but he'd gotten to see that side of her, and still wanted to get to know her better.

Aiden's back was to her, as she rounded the bottom of the stairs, and her heart jumped at the sight of those broad shoulders. Her pussy clenched suddenly, and she was back in her bed the previous night, coming on her fingers, wishing they were his. She stopped and hid for a moment, taking a breath and trying to collect herself.

She could do this.

"Hey Aiden."

His smile when he saw her, lit her up from the inside, and she teetered on the step for a moment.

"Hey there Lillie. Wow, you look great!" He came to the bottom of the stairs and offered her his hand as she stepped down. She felt his touch all the way down to her toes.

"Thank you. You look pretty great yourself." He really did. Aiden's hair was swept back in a manbun, leaving the strong lines of his face clear, and she wanted to trace them with her fingers, before loosing his hair so it could fall about her as he leaned above her.

She squeaked, and almost died when he looked at her questioningly. "No no, I'm good."

"You're better than good." His grin was infectious. "Now, why don't you message Ralphie now, so he knows I've picked you up, and we'll be on our way?"

The air outside was cold and biting, and Lillie hugged her coat around her tight as they walked towards his car. And then he opened the door for her, helped her sweep her long coat in, so it didn't get caught in the door, and leaned across her to snick her seatbelt into place. She got a whiff of him, and she was glad he hadn't worn any aftershave. Aftershave and perfumes were sensory nightmares, but also, this way she got to smell him, and he was all woodsy and musky. Lillie had to stop herself from leaning in and taking a deep sniff.

"You smell nice."

The words left her mouth before she could stop herself, and she rolled her eyes to cover her discomfort. "I'm sorry, I'm autistic and really not very good with filters sometimes."

"Why would I mind that you're saying something nice

about me? That's totally okay." He leaned in to kiss her cheek. "You smell nice too."

She lifted her hand to her cheek as he walked around to the driver's side, revelling in the brief touch of his lips. They were soft, and the stubble of his beard wasn't scratchy at all, though she wondered if that would be the kiss on soft skin between her thighs.

Flushing, she shook her head, trying to pull herself together some more. *Focus Lillie. Dinner and getting to know each other. Not sex.* But there was a part of her that really *really* wanted sex to be on the table.

"You know," he said, as he pulled away from her apartment building, "if you'd feel comfortable with it, you don't have to mask around me, or constantly explain the way you do things. I'll say if I don't understand something, but as a rule, unless you're being intentionally mean, I'm rather laid back. You are you, and that's fine with me."

It was a lot of words aimed at Lillie, and a lot aimed specifically at the thing that made her different, the thing that she'd been told made her unlovable. Her too muchness; her high levels of enthusiasm; her spates of very low energy levels; all of the things made her different and unique and special to some people, had been the reason she'd been rejected by others.

That was okay. She'd come to terms with the fact that not everyone was going to love her, but she did deserve to have people who welcomed her as she was. And she liked that Aiden didn't shy away from the fact that she was different.

Because she was different. It's what allowed her to hyperfocus to the point that she could talk about the production and upkeep of hundreds of different types of fabrics, that allowed her to remember all of the things that brought her friends joy, or made them stressed. She remembered details that everyone else forgot, and that could be so damn handy sometimes.

"It does mean that I'm not always comfortable round lots of people, but I can self-regulate; I've gotten pretty good at that."

He nodded, "That makes sense. Is there anything that you really don't like?"

Lillie thought hard. "I really don't like aftershave or perfumes; they're really overpowering and make me flinch a bit. But I can cope with gentle scents in shampoo or deodorants. And I don't like not knowing the rules."

"The rules?" he quirked an eyebrow at her, and she giggled.

"Not *those* kinds of rules, though I suppose those as well, but mainly the rules of a place or people. Every person has these unspoken rules that everyone else is expected to know, and I find that really stressful. And it means that when there's a big social event, often it's sensory overload because I'm expected to know the rules for multiple people all at once. That's why I stuck to the blankets at the munch – I knew what the people there expected."

"That sounds pretty tiring." Aiden's voice wasn't critical, just curious, and that was a good sign. People who tried to argue with her about how she processed things usually weren't people she liked to spend any time around.

"Oh it's *exhausting*. That's why I don't go out out very often. I spend time with a couple of friends, at work, and with my family too, but big groups are too much most of the time." She looked at him nervously. "Is where you tell me that you have a million and one friends, and that if we started to date, you'd want me to spend time with them all constantly?"

He laughed, "No no. I do have a large number of friends, but most of the time we do small catch ups, in couples or groups of four or five. How would you feel about that?"

Lillie drummed her fingers on the car seat's armrest as she thought. "I could probably do that, depending on the setting and the activity. It's usually handy if there's somewhere I can go to take a break, if I have to. But I have a big family and they do big parties that I've just had to adjust to."

"And how do you adjust to those?"

She laughed. "To be honest, its where being a secret Little kind of comes in handy. I end up being in charge of all the kids, and running the craft table or organising games. And it's brilliant because children don't expect you to mask, and see stimming as just an extension of play. It's really rather lovely."

"Well, that sounds just adorable. And also, really smart."

Lillie beamed. That fluttery feeling in her tummy was back, the good fluttery feeling that made her want to do a happy dance. Her fingers picked up speed on the armrest as they turned into the parking lot of the restaurant.

He'd picked a really fancy restaurant, she realised as she got out of the car. One with the kind of very simple, muted logo that promised delicious food at unreasonable prices.

"Oh, I'm not really sure this is in my budget."

He came round the car and leaned against it. "Well, I asked you out for dinner, so I was hoping you'd let me treat you. Would that be okay?"

When Lillie nodded, he offered her his hand, intertwining their fingers when she accepted. There was a small part of her that wanted to be Little, and swing their arms together, but the warmth of his palm against hers—that skin-to-skin contact that she'd been longing for all day—made her want to pull him close and kiss him.

She looked at his lips as they entered the restaurant and spoke to the maître d'. They looked strong, firm and like they'd be just the lips that could kiss her senseless.

He caught her staring, and just smiled and led her over to their table, pulling out her chair for her and going full gentleman date. Though she'd kind of revelled in the way his eyes had widened when she'd taken off her coat, revealing her dress. And then her skirt might have shown off the tops of her stockings when she sat down, before she was able to rearrange it of course. Looking up, Lillie saw a twinkle in his eyes that made her laugh.

"You look very very pretty tonight."

"I do rather, don't I?" She wasn't entirely certain where the sass came from, but it made him laugh as he sat down.

"You very much do."

The menu was full of the kind of Italian food that always made her mouth water, and she ummed and ahhed until settling on tortellini en brodo.

"So," Aiden said, pouring her some water. "how did you find the munch the other evening? It was your first time, right?"

She took a sip and nodded. "My first time at that munch, yes. I've been to others before. And it was really fun! I liked that there was colouring set out; made it less intimidating, talking to all the people standing around."

"Yeah, there's a good mix of Littles and Middles and Caregivers there," he said. "And the organisers apparently learnt early on that if they didn't have a Little space, some people just found it too intimidating to attend. And because it's in a private room, it's not problematic for other people in the pub."

"That makes sense. How did you find out that you were a Daddy Dom?" Her voice dropped on the last two words and she looked around cautiously. Lillie didn't usually talk so openly like this, but if she could talk about her stimming with Aiden, then she could definitely talk about this.

"I started off as a pleasure Dom really, and then had one

or two encounters that made me realise that the caregiving aspect of being a Daddy Dom really appealed to me. But it's not something I take lightly. I haven't had a Little of my own for quite a long time."

"A pleasure Dom?" Lillie's head swum a bit. A pleasure Dom sounded…

"That's right. There's nothing I love more than…" he paused as she ducked her head to hide her blushes. "Are you sure you're okay with talking about that side of things Lillie? It's okay if you're not?"

"Oh no! I definitely am!" She almost stumbled over her words in her need to explain. "I just sometimes get a bit shy, is all."

Aiden leaned across the table to tuck her hair behind her ear. "Getting shy is totally okay, sweetheart, but I need you to be able to communicate with me if you're not sure about something."

"Would traffic lights work?" She'd used them before and simple words like that seemed like a much simpler way of pausing something than having to try and work out what she wanted to say, especially if she was feeling the overwhelm.

"Traffic lights work beautifully. Do you have much experience with them?"

They paused as their first course came. Lillie did a happy dance as she tried her pasta; strong delicious flavours in the tortellini, combined with that deliciously warming chicken broth. He noticed her wiggle and smiled that delicious smile that made her want to dance all over again.

"It's really good."

"Apparently so."

She took another spoonful before answering. "I used traffic lights with my ex, and I also tap out sometimes, if I go non-verbal from overstimulation." She shot a look up at him that she knew was slightly teasing. "Have you ever done overstimulation play?"

"Have I ever…baby girl, there's nothing I like more than making a sub come apart for me, over and over and over." He didn't force her to meet his eyes, almost as if he knew that that might be too much for her, but she could tell that he was watching her reaction closely.

Her very instinctive reaction.

She squeaked.

Lillie didn't squeak all that often, and she'd been assured before that it was adorable when she did, but she just didn't know how to process that in front of a potential Daddy.

He ran his hand across the top of his head and have a short, deep chuckle. "Damn, Lillie. Many more squeaks like that, and I'll be wanting to see what other noises you can make."

"Or what other noises you can draw out of me." This time she did meet his gaze long enough to see his eyes darken with an intensity that made her almost wriggle with impatience in her chair."

"Dinner first. Talks. And then we can see." Aiden's voice was stern, but kind. "And that's as much for my self-control as it is for yours."

She nodded and dove back into her soup. "What do you like most about being a Daddy Dom?"

"Can I say everything?" They laughed together, and then he continued. "No, seriously, I think it's about the fact that I want the person I'm with to feel completely safe and happy, and if I can help them create a space where they can feel those feelings, then that's amazing. Plus, cartoons. Littles think that their caregivers only watch cartoons because they ask them to, but secretly we love watching them too."

That made her gurgle with laughter. "Oh yes? What's your favourite?"

"I mean, there's the classic Disney fare, but I do have a soft spot for Bee and Puppycat."

Lillie nodded seriously. "An excellent choice. And it's good for Little space or Big space really."

He inclined his head in agreement. "Definitely. So, what do you like most about being a Little, and what would you want from a Daddy Dom, Lillie?"

$$\text{\Large 6}$$

Oh. So they were asking the important questions now. Lillie paused to think. What did she want?

She'd had a lot of time to think about it since her breakup, almost putting her Little away for a year. It was only with the job at Stuffie Hospital that she really let herself indulge in the smallest of Little moments: watching cartoons on occasion; carrying a stuffie client round with her at work; drinking chocolate milk—because no matter what happened, she didn't think she'd ever be able to give up choccie milk.

"I think," she said slowly, "that I'm clearer about what I don't want, and about what my limits are."

"That's really good," said Aiden, "Knowing your limits is vital in any dynamic. And it's particularly important for a Little, as you're so vulnerable." The kindness in his voice made her look up. "Do you feel comfortable sharing those limits with me sweetheart?"

Lillie took a deep breath. "Yes, I think it's important for me to do so. I haven't always been very good at communicating my needs, and it's one of the things that I can't budge on going forward."

She had some more of her soup, collecting her thoughts, before explaining. This was important, so she didn't want to get it wrong. She liked Aiden too much for that.

"I'm a non-sexual Little; that's my first boundary. When I'm Little, I want to watch cartoons and eat kids' food and have all of the cosy cuddles, but nothing more than that. It's Big me that likes the grown-up things." She blushed a bit at that. "And I like lots of the grown-up things. Just not in that space."

Aiden nodded seriously. "That's what I want from a dynamic too."

Okay. So that bit went down well. "I also need to be myself. That means that I need to be able to stim, and sometimes I need to be able to retreat without getting punished for it. It's not that I'm refusing to communicate, just that sometimes I get so overwhelmed that I can't."

Looking up, she realised that he'd taken out a notebook, and was jotting down some notes. "What are you doing?"

"Oh, don't worry sweetheart, I'm just making some notes so I don't forget anything. But your name isn't mentioned at all. It's just that this seems like it's very important to you, so it's important to me."

"Okay." That made her feel…safe. Her pulse, which had rocketed when she'd noticed the notebook, settled back down and her fingers went back to drumming happily on her knee. Happy stimming. Safe stimming. "And rules are nice, and good, but I need to negotiate them. I really dislike it when someone gives me a rule 'just because'."

He paused his writing for a moment. "What happens if I were to suggest a rule that you didn't like."

Lillie thought about it for a moment. "I think it would depend on what it was, and why you were suggesting it. I might suggest a trial, with the option to safe out? Because if you were my Daddy Dom—" Her voice cut out suddenly. *My*

Daddy Dom. How long had it been since she'd said those words?

"Are you okay sweetheart?"

She shook her head and continued. "Yes, thank you. If you were my Daddy Dom, then I'd assume that you had my best interests at heart. But not all Doms do, so I need some protection too."

"I'm really proud of you, Lillie."

Her heart jumped up into her throat, and for a moment she thought that she might cry. "Why?"

"Because it's not easy to know that you need to look after yourself, especially when you're a Little. But I hope that if we decide to pursue this dynamic, you'll come to trust me completely. I'd never do anything to abuse your faith in me."

"Okay." Her voice was small. It had been so long since someone had told her that they were proud of her. But it wasn't even just the words, it was the fact that he was the one who'd said them. He saw *her* and he was proud of *her*. That meant the world.

"Are there any other limits for you?"

"No gags please, or humiliation. I spent enough time being silenced or insulted."

And there was that look in his eyes again, the same look he'd had when she told him that she didn't need stuffies. It was unwavering.

"No one gets to silence you or insult you again. Not even you. Is that understood, Lillie?"

She looked at him. "Is that a rule?"

Aiden sighed. "If we were to agree to a dynamic, I'd like to have a version of that as a rule. That you always tell me if anyone attempts to silence you or insults you, so that I can make sure that you are safe and that you process that properly. And that you try your best not to silence or insult yourself. I know sometimes it's not easy, but I won't have anyone hurting my little one. Not even herself. What do you think?"

Lillie's face warmed as he said 'my little one'. She wanted him to say those words to her intentionally, saying that she was his little one. His brown eyes met hers. "I think that sounds reasonable."

"I'm glad. And you've said the things that you don't want, and your boundaries, but not much about what you *do* want. What do you need from a caregiver?"

She wasn't sure she'd ever been asked that before. She'd been asked what she liked, but never really what she needed. "Affection, please. Lots of it. Pet names, and cuddles, and looking after me. And stories. I really really need stories."

"I remember you mentioning your Little books before; why are stories so important to you?"

She'd wondered that herself before, crushed as she had been by her ex's refusal to read to her. "I think it's because I can lose myself in a story. Curled up under blankets, with someone's arms around me, reading to me, showing me the pictures… It's a different world. A safe world."

"Well, I would love to tuck you up in bed and read to you, little one."

Lillie did a happy wriggle. "Yes please. What would you expect from your Little?" She almost called him Daddy, but just about held the honorific back.

"I would expect that they communicated with me openly and truthfully. That they let me spoil them sometimes, but also that if they did something that they knew to be wrong, they'd submit to an agreed upon punishment."

"A punishment?"

"I've always found spankings to be effective."

Lillie's bum tingled, as if in anticipation. "Like in a release kind of way?"

"Exactly. I don't like giving punishments, but sometimes

Littles need a reset, and then it's really important to do something that allows them to let go of the bad feelings that comes with breaking a rule, and move on."

She nodded slowly. "That makes sense I think, even if the idea is a bit scary."

"Bad scary?"

It wasn't a bad scary, not really. In fact, it almost made her feel better, knowing that he'd actually care if she broke a rule. That felt solid. "I don't think so."

"And of course, there's what you called the grown-up things. Little you is adorable Lillie, but Big you is gorgeous, and I'd want to show you just how gorgeous I think you are. How does that sound?"

"Like making me come apart over and over?" His eyes darkened as she said his own words back to him.

"Well aren't you being cheeky?"

"Only a little bit!"

He laughed. "That's okay, I like cheeky. Now, at the munch you said something about honorifics. Would you like to continue that conversation now?"

She nodded enthusiastically. "How would you feel if I called you Daddy?"

Aiden leaned forward to take her hand in his, running his thumb over the backs of her fingers until she almost couldn't think straight. He noticed her glazed eyes and paused the stroking for a moment. "Oh sweetheart, you are too adorable. If you'd like to explore this dynamic with me, I'd love for you to call me Daddy. What would you like me to call you?"

"I like little one," she said, and then, more hesitantly, "and babygirl?"

"Little one and babygirl it is," he said. "With the occasional sweetheart thrown in for good measure – especially when round other people."

"That sounds lovely." It really did. Lillie's whole body was fizzing with excitement now, and wriggled in her chair again, to let some of the fizz out.

"Your wriggles are so adorable, babygirl. You all good?"

"Yes, thank you." She beamed up at him. "I think…I mean…I would like…if you don't mind…" Taking a breath, Lillie stopped and pulled her words back together. "This food has been delicious, but I have ice cream at mine, if you'd like to…"

"I've never known a Little not to have ice cream at home," he laughed. "And I would love to, if you're sure that's what you want. We don't have to rush into anything."

When she looked at him this time, she let all of the desire and affection she felt for him flood her eyes. "I don't feel like we're rushing, Daddy."

He swore under his breath, and signalled over to the waitress for the bill. "Babygirl, you're going to be the death of me."

After leaving the restaurant, she paused as he opened the car door for her, tugging at his hand. "Ummm…Daddy?"

"Yes, babygirl?"

"Do you think maybe we should," she dropped her voice, "kiss? Just to make sure that there's, you know, a spark?"

"Well don't I have the smartest babygirl? I think you're right; we definitely should kiss." And then he was leaning down to brush his lips against hers.

One, two, gentle brushes, but before he could pull back, she held onto his collar and tugged him back towards her, moulding her body and mouth to his until she was no longer entirely certain where she ended and he began.

It was the kind of kiss that dreams were made of, the kind of kiss that would have set off fireworks in a movie.

He cupped her face with his hands and walked her back until her back was against the car, and she whimpered into his mouth as he plundered hers. Her knees weakened, and then he was wrapping one arm around her tightly, holding her so tightly that she thought if she'd swooned, he wouldn't even need to move to catch her.

When they came up for air, his breathing was staccato, and her voice jagged.

"I think there's a spark Daddy."

☙   7   ❧

As soon as they entered the door of her apartment, it felt as if there were a thousand hands between the two of them, teasing, touching, pulling. When he took her hair down, and fisted his hand in Lillie's curls, she moaned.

Her turn. Tugging at the band in his hair until it released, soft, silky waves cascaded down. Lillie ran her fingers through them and laughed in delight. "I love your hair Daddy."

"Oh yeah?" His voice had deepened, darkened by the desire that was painted across his face. "Imagine how it'll look across your thighs as I eat you out."

She squeaked, and he chuckled then.

"Would that be okay, babygirl?"

Would it be okay? It was all Lillie could do to prevent herself from throwing herself on the sofa and begging him to have his way with her. "Yes, that's totally okay Daddy."

Pausing quickly to hang her coat up, she took his hand and led him to her bedroom, grateful that at least her and Ralphie had tidied away the discarded possible outfits.

Oh! Ralphie!

"Ummm…is it okay if I text Ralphie?"

He pulled her close and kissed her. "You should definitely text Ralphie. Good girl for remembering."

"I like it when you call me good girl."

"Keeping on being so good, and you'll see what kind of rewards I have lined for such a good girl."

"Rewards?" Her eyes widened and he laughed.

"Go message Ralphie now, and then come here so I can take all your clothes off, you gorgeous creature."

She skidded round the corner, almost falling over in her hurry to get to her phone. Pulling it out of her coat pocket, she sent off a quick message and waited for the reply.

LILLIE: *The restaurant was lovely. Lots of yummy food. We're back at mine now.*

Ralphie: WE?!

Lillie: Yes. I think I also have a Daddy…

Ralphie: THIS IS EXCITING NEWS. I WANT TO KNOW EVERYTHING.

Ralphie: But also, go have fun! And be safe! And text me before you go to sleep, so I know that it all went okay?

Lillie: I will!!! Thank you!!

"ALL DONE!" she sang as she rounded her bedroom door to see her Daddy sat on the bed, taking off his shirt.

"I hope you don't mind, babygirl, but I thought I'd get a little comfortable."

The only thing that Lillie minded was the fact that she hadn't had the chance to take his shirt off herself. "Mind? Not in the slightest!"

She bounced over to the bed, and he pulled her onto her

lap, until she was straddling his thighs. Her skirt rode up and he ran a hand through his hair as he saw her stockings.

"I thought I saw a glimpse of stockings at the restaurant, but I wasn't sure…"

"Oh, you mean these?" And with a brazenness that she didn't know she had, Lillie slowly pulled up her skirt, revealing inch after inch of black stockings until she hit the tops of her thighs and froze.

The kiss that followed was reassurance itself. "Yes, I meant those stockings, sweetheart. They're very sexy, just like you. But it's okay if you get a bit shy about showing me everything, I can help with that if you like?"

Lillie nodded enthusiastically. "Yes please! I want to, but sometimes I get all…" she hid her face in his shoulder, and he chuckled and stroked her hair.

"I understand babygirl. Why don't you try again?"

She nuzzled against his hand and then straightened up, lowering her eyes until she raised her skirt until he could see the black lacy knickers that hid beneath.

"Well, aren't you good, dressing up all pretty for me?" The touch of his hands on her knees, made her wriggle, and he groaned. "Damn babygirl." Because she could feel him now, hard and insistent beneath his trousers, pressing up between her thighs.

She wriggled again, experimentally, and he gave her a smart rap on her arse. "Ow!"

"Behave yourself, Lillie." It was the first time he'd used his Dom voice on her, and it made her go all melty. As if someone had flicked a switch in her brain, and now she was in full on sub mode.

"Yes Sir."

He grinned at the honorific, and then tugged at her hair until her neck was bared for him. "I. Love. You. All. Dressed. Up. For. Me" Each word was punctuated with a kiss or a nip or a lick that made her almost mewl in pleasure. "But," and here he nipped and sucked at the point where her neck met her shoulder until she almost melted into a puddle in his arms, "I think I'd like to see you undressed a little bit more."

Standing on shaky legs, Lillie stood up, and slowly untied the halter neck of her dress, looking down as the fabric rustled and then pooled around her ankles. Stepping out, she peeked at him from under her lashes. His gaze felt like a touch, caressing every inch of her skin, lingering over the swell of her hips, and the curve of her stomach. She'd never felt more desirable than in that moment.

He stood up and pulled her flush against him, one hand curved round the nape of her neck. "You are beautiful babygirl. Now get on the bed."

Blinking, she crawled onto the bed, squeaking as he grabbed her feet and flipped her over.

"Bra off please babygirl."

She obeyed as he moved to kneel above her on the bed, bracketing her with his arms, before leaning down to take one nipple in his mouth.

Lillie almost arched off the bed.

His mouth was teasing, alternating between kissing and sucking and gentle biting at her breast, and each time she moaned, it only made him do so more.

"Stroke yourself for me," he whispered in her ear, as he moved to her right breast, and when Lillie reached down to feel between her legs, she found that her knickers were sodden. The heat from her pussy radiated through the material, and then she was pulling them to one side and sighing as she ran her fingers between her lips and up to her clit.

She trembled beneath his mouth, and ran her other hand through his hair, desperate to hold on to something as the pressure between her legs built.

And then his mouth was gone, the air cool against her exposed nipple. She felt almost bereft at the loss of it, at least until his lips kissed her inner thigh.

"How do you feel about coming apart for me, babygirl?"

"Wha-what?"

"Use your words please, sweetness. Tell me how you need me."

She almost came apart then, his words filling her the way that words hadn't in far too long, but she stopped circling her clit with her thumb, and forced herself to meet his eyes. "Can you lick me please Daddy? I'd like to come apart beneath your mouth."

"Well, since you asked so very nicely…"

When he pulled her knickers down her legs, she was grateful that she'd taken the time to pull them up over her stockings earlier. And then his face was *there*, and he was stroking and teasing and oh good *grief* that felt good.

"Oh please Daddy, please." She reached out, and there his hair was, spilling over her thighs, just like he'd promised and she thought she'd never seen anything so beautiful.

He lapped at her pussy first, as if determined to get every last drop of her wetness, before licking up until he could suck her clit into his mouth. It was oh so much, almost too much, and moaned and writhed beneath his mouth. When he chuckled this time, she felt it *everywhere*.

"How you doing there, babygirl?"

Her fingers fluttered against her thighs, and then she was stroking his hair, over and over, as if touching, touching him would stop her from floating away altogether. "M-more please, Daddy. If that's okay?"

"More?" his words were teasing, but she didn't feel self-conscious. All that mattered was him and her.

"Can you, can you fill me up please?"

He took her clit in his mouth again and sucked hard as he

slid a finger into her, half laughing as she bucked beneath him. "You like that?"

"Yes yes, oh *please* yes."

"I like please, babygirl. And you have been so very good, so how about I…"

Lillie wasn't entirely what he did next, some kind of Daddy magic with his fingers, that had her crying out louder than she thought she'd ever done before. And then she was clenching and tightening, and then, with one more whispered "please", she fell into waterfalling pleasure where nothing existed but his hands and his mouth and his hair covering her like a blanket of stars.

When she came to, he was holding her in his arms, kissing her every time an aftershock ran through her body. "You did so well, babygirl. I'm so proud of you."

She leaned and kissed him, smiling at the taste of her on his lips. "Thank you, Daddy. But I'd like to…" she reached down towards the front of his trousers, and then paused, "If that's okay?"

Standing up, he pulled his belt off, snapping the leather tight in his hands, and then laughing at how wide her eyes got. "Not today, babygirl. But another time, I promise." And then he was undressing and finally, *finally*, she got see his cock.

It was hard, which she'd already guessed, but she could see precum glistening at the tip, and she crawled forward to the edge of the bed, and licked it off. "Yum. You taste so nice Daddy."

He groaned, and then gently took her head in his hands, and nudged her forward again.

When she took him in her mouth, she loved how he felt beneath her tongue, velvet over steel. Swirling her tongue around his tip, she urged herself to take him deep and deeper until she was bobbing her head up and down, his cock hitting the entrance to her throat each time.

But he didn't let her suck him for too long. She almost whined when he pulled her head off him, and he leaned down to kiss her. "I want to fill another of your holes, babygirl."

And then she was on all fours, arse up in the air, and his fingers were back stroking her entrance, gathering her wetness and slipping in and out, stretching her in preparation for his cock.

Then unrelenting emptiness whilst during the tearing of foil, and then he was back, nudging at her entrance until she pushed back and took all of him in one fell movement.

It was almost overwhelming at first. It had been so long since she'd been fucked that she'd forgotten how totally full it made her feel, and when he bottomed out in her pussy her moans became an incoherent stream of nonsense that she had no control over. Just moaning and babbling and begging him for more and faster and Daddy until he was pounding her tight pussy over and over. And then his fingers were slipping beneath her to touch her button and she was gone. Shattering again and again as he moved in her, around her, holding her, pressing at her, caressing her, fucking her.

He came with a shout, and as he spent himself, he enveloped her in his arms.

Lillie's cheeks were wet, and she didn't even realise that she'd been crying until he turned her over and kissed them gently away.

"Are you okay, my sweet girl?"

"Yes, Daddy," she whispered.

"Would you like me to stay with you?"

She nodded vigorously. "Please Daddy, please don't leave me tonight," and then he was picking her up and holding her in his lap, rocking her back and forth and muttering sweet praise in her ear, until she calmed.

"Would you like some water?"

"Yes please. And I need to," she gestured towards the bathroom.

"Of course."

When she got back, her phone was on her bedside table, so that she could check in with Ralphie, next to a glass of water, and there was a book on her bed.

"I know you've been all Big, but I was wondering if you'd like a story before we go to sleep. We don't have to—"

Lillie launched herself at him, and hugged him hard. "That would be amazing." He tucked her up in bed, putting his arms around her and pulling her close, as he read a story of a bear who loved marmalade sandwiches ever so much. And then her Daddy turned off the light, pulled her into his arms, so she fit just right, and cuddled her until she fell asleep.

❧   8   ❧

Lillie floated through work the next day. She'd woken to more kisses and cuddles, and a rather hot and steamy shower, before they'd both had to rush out the door to head to work.

He kept sending her adorable texts throughout the day, and little reminders to have a snack, or eat her lunch, or have some water.

She liked those kinds of reminders; made her feel cared for and looked after, and she'd been practically dancing when she told Ralphie all about the previous night.

Having a Daddy was the best, she decided. Or at least, having Aiden as her Daddy was the best. Orgasms *and* stories? I mean, what more could a sub ask for?

So she was a little taken aback when she saw him after lunch, heading towards Rebecca's restoration station.

"Hey Aiden," she said, bounding over, and only just remembering not to call him Daddy in front of people outside their dynamic. "How are you?"

"Good thanks Lillie." His smile was polite, and there was none of the teasing warmth that she expected to see. "I've got to ask Rebecca some questions about some restoration techniques for the article."

"I can help with that, if you like?"

He looked down at her, shifting from foot to foot. "Thank you, but this really is something that only Rebecca can do."

"Oh, okay."

That seemed odd. Rebecca had been here longer, but there was no seniority or hierarchy amongst the restoration specialists; they both did exactly the same job.

"It's just a flying visit." Pausing, he leaned down until he could meet her eyes. "Are you okay, Lillie?"

"Yes, thank you." Her words were as polite as his smile had been, and there was nothing in her tone that indicated the turmoil she felt inside.

"Okay then, I'll see you later."

She watched as he walked over to Rebecca's station, and then turned away, her eyes burning.

It didn't make any sense. She could have answered any questions he'd had, but maybe... The scrunch hit her extra hard this time, and she gasped, hurriedly walking out of the room, and heading for the stock cupboard. That would probably be empty right now, and she need a space, any space, where she could get her scrunch under control.

It hadn't felt this bad in a long time, not since her ex had told her that he hadn't wanted her any more, that she was too much.

This was that feeling.

Was that what had happened there? That Daddy, that *Aiden*, had had some fun the night before, but now that it was over, it was awkward?

Her pulse was raising, her mouth dry and she almost heaved as she rushed into the stock cupboard.

She leant her head against the cold metal of the shelves, needing something to break her out of the cycle that was threatening to overwhelm her. No no no. This wasn't happening. This couldn't be happening. Aiden was lovely, and communicated. He'd read her a *story*. He wouldn't just…

"Lillie?"

When she turned around, she was hyperventilating now, and the stock manager, Warren, didn't say a word. He just pulled out a chair from goodness only knew where, sat her down, and made her copy his breathing until hers evened out.

She was still shaking though, and he put his jacket around her shoulders. "Oh kiddo, you poor thing. What happened?"

"Nothing. Nothing, I'm fine."

There was a silence, and when she looked up, he looked unimpressed. "Fine?"

"Okay, maybe not fine, but it's a panic attack. Just a scrunch. Nothing to take to seriously, just my brain overthinking and overwhelming me. It's nothing." And the thing was that Lillie knew, deep down, she *knew* that her Daddy wasn't abandoning her. There was a perfectly good explanation for everything, if only she'd thought to ask.

"Perhaps you should go home. Get some rest. I'll let Miss Owens know."

Her legs were wobbly when she made her way back into the main studio, hands trembling a little as she pushed her hair back off her face, and gathered her things together.

"Lillie?" Aiden's face was all concern. "What happened?"

"I'm okay, I'm fine," she began, but Aiden looked at her bag questioningly.

"You're going home?"

She clenched her fists and unclenched them rapidly, trying to stave off another scrunch. "Yeah, I had a…I had a moment. Warren said I should probably go home."

"I'll take you."

"It's okay, I–"

"Lillie." Aiden's voice brooked no discussion. "I'm taking you home. Give me your bag please."

Hanging her head, she did as she was told, gathering up her things and wrapping her scarf round her so many times she could barely incline her head. Being wrapped tight always made her feel better.

He didn't speak much in the car, but insisted on taking her up to her apartment, and making her something to eat.

"I'm fine," she tried to insist.

"Lillie. If you lie to me one more time about being fine, you will be in even more trouble than you're already in."

That put a stop to her protests immediately.

She sat quietly whilst he made her what looked like the fanciest grilled cheese sandwich that she'd ever seen, and he sat with her whilst she ate it, topping up her water, and merely raising an eyebrow when she said she wasn't thirsty. Lillie drank it all.

When she was done, he cleared her plate and did the washing up, pointing her towards her couch when she offered to help.

Waiting for him to finish tidying up was not fun, and she hated the fact that he wasn't really talking to her, but when he sat down next to her on the couch, he didn't look angry, just disappointed.

That was worse.

"I know we hadn't put many rules in place, little one, but what was the one thing I said I expected."

"That I'm kind to myself?"

"And...?"

"That I communicate with you."

"Exactly. Now, when I asked you earlier if you were okay, and you said that you were, were you telling me the truth?"

"Kind of..." Aiden looked at her and Lillie squirmed in her seat. "Well, my head got a bit funny and anxious, and I know that that's just my head being funny and anxious—it's got nothing to do with anything you did, exactly. It didn't seem worth bothering you with."

"Lillie, if you're going to my little girl, then you need to understand that if I ask you how you are, it's because I actually want to know the answer. You don't help me or yourself if you're not truthful with me. If you'd told me, then maybe you wouldn't have had to have a panic attack."

Her fingers were trembling, and she couldn't even bring herself to drum them across her knees, she was so upset. He sounded so *ad*. She didn't want her Daddy to sound sad. That was *awful*.

Her eyes welled up with tears that threatened to drown her in regrets. "I'm sorry, Daddy."

"I know you are babygirl, but you need to understand that I'm not going to be angry with you for being anxious. And that I can't help you, if I don't know what's wrong. So. What happened?"

"You didn't want to talk to me!" Her voice wobbled and she grabbed a cushion to hold onto as she started to cry. "I know that it's silly, and there is a perfectly good reason, but I couldn't shake the feeling that I'd done something wrong, that you didn't want me anymore." And then he was holding her in his arms as she cried.

"Oh babygirl, if you'd only told me… Wait there."

He went and grabbed his bag from where he'd left against the doorframe, and opened it up, pulling out the most adorable white unicorn stuffie. It had a pink horn and hooves, and a rainbow main and tail and Lillie almost choked on her tears.

"I was asking Rebecca to make sure that I'd sewn up the hole that it had properly. I've never fixed a stuffie before."

Lillie sat silently, looking between Aiden and the unicorn, completely confused. "I don't understand."

"I promised you I'd find you a stuffie, babygirl, and I did. She's yours." He held him out to her, and Lillie dropped the cushion in her eagerness to hold her.

"She's so soft Daddy!"

"I know she is, babygirl, and that's why I was speaking to Rebecca. And if you'd only told me how you were feeling, I'd have been able to put your mind at ease."

She started crying again. This felt *horrible*. Not only had she broken a rule, but not telling the truth, but she'd not trusted her Daddy when all along he was doing the sweetest thing in the world for her. "I'm a terrible Little. How could I be so awful?" she said, in between sobs.

"Enough, Lillie. I was going to let it go, because this was your first time, but you know you're not allowed to be mean about yourself like that." Her Daddy's voice was stern, and she curled up on the couch and sniffled.

"I'm sorry."

"I know you are, but you know what the rules are, don't you?"

"Spanks?"

"Spanks."

Lillie's stomach dropped, and her bottom lip started trembling again.

"Now, would you can hold your stuffie if you like, but spanks are happening, babygirl."

"Okay." She followed Aiden meekly into her bedroom, her stuffie firmly grasped in her arms, and then looked at him for guidance.

He sat down, and patted his lap. "Over here, little one."

She shuffled over, refusing to make eye contact, and meekly arranging herself over his knee. Did she want spanks? Not like this. Fun grown up spanks? Sure, but not because she'd disappointed Daddy. That was the worst.

"I'm only going to give you twenty—"

"Twenty?!" Lillie couldn't help her outburst, and hushed as soon as she saw the look on his face.

"Yes Lillie. Twenty. Because you lied to me and then you were mean about yourself. And you're going to count them off for me as well."

"Yes Daddy."

He flipped her skirt up around her waist, and then pulled her knickers down to her knees. "You ready, babygirl?"

She squeezed her eyes shut as tight as she could, and clung onto her new stuffie. "No!"

"Lillie?"

"Okay, okay. Yes Daddy, I'm ready."

The first one sounded worse than it felt, a sharp smack that fell across her right cheek. It made her squeal, but she was able to count it. "One, sorry Daddy."

He paused, and then gently corrected her. "Thank you Daddy, not sorry Daddy. We're doing this so that you can let go of all those big feels around this, and we can move on. And we can't do that if you're still apologising the whole way through."

She sniffled. "Okay Daddy."

The second across her left cheek, but after that he picked up both the speed and the weight behind it until she was kicking her legs and sobbing into her stuffie's mane.

Lillie wailed the last count, "Twenty, thank you Daddy," and then just fell apart completely, crying her eyes out.

Her Daddy picked her up, and carried her into the bathroom, where he held her on his lap, kissing her forehead, and stroking her hair whilst he ran a bath. "Oh, little one, I'm so so proud of you. That was really hard, but it's all over now, it's all gone. You don't have to worry anymore. You did so so well."

He placed her stuffie on the side and helped her stand up

and undress, before gently settling her into a bath full of sparkles and bubble bath foam.

The warmth of the water seeped into her bones until she felt warm and rosy all over, her breathing evening out as she lay back and allowed herself to float in the water—which also had the unexpected benefit of taking the pressure off her sore bottom.

"Daddy?"

"Yes babygirl?"

"Are you still cross with me?"

He knelt down beside the bath, and stroked her hair. "Of course not sweetness, and I was never really *cross*. I understand that sometimes you need to retreat, but you can't lie to me about why you're retreating or how you're feeling. And you're not allowed to be so mean about yourself. I care about you, so I need you to care about you too."

She nodded slowly, "I think that makes sense. And usually I don't like crying, but that crying wasn't because of overwhelm or my scrunch, it was because I made you sad."

"Your scrunch?"

"That funny feeling you get when everything feels wrong and panicky."

"Ah, I see." He stood up and opened a towel out for her, giving her a hand out of the bath. She giggled as he towelled her dry vigorously, though he was extra careful across her bottom. "Right, cuddles in bed, and maybe a story?"

"Yes please Daddy." And as she padded across the room, her new stuffie in one hand, and her Daddy's hand in the other, she realised that she was safe. He had her, and he was never going to let her go.

A Little's REINDEER

ELLIE ROSE

❦ 9 ❦

Tuesdays were Georgie Dunbar's favourite day of the week.

Yes, he had weekends off, and his weekends were often very pleasant indeed, but his weekends weren't filled with the gruffness of Warren Freeman.

Georgie got to drive all over with his job, sourcing vintage toy parts from all over the country for different collectors and restoration specialists, and for the most part that meant seeing different people every single day. But since Stuffie Hospital had opened a few years previously, he'd ended up going over there every Tuesday.

Friday night, Warren would email his stock list over—always the most professional, to the point, missives—and every Friday night Georgie would bounce in his chair when he got the email, and then start counting down the hours to when he'd get to see Warren in person.

There was something deliciously satisfying about bounding into the stock cupboard and prattling away as he made his delivery.

And for all of Warren's gruffness, there was always a cup

of cocoa waiting for Georgie. Georgie thought he liked that more than everything else about Warren put together. Yes, the older man was tall and handsome, with a dark beard and forearms that Georgie had to steadfastly ignore, in case his brain overloaded, but he was also quietly kind.

Georgie hadn't really had quietly kind before.

He'd had loud and posturing, and he'd had angry, and he'd even had mean, but quietly kind men seemed to never quite make it into his orbit.

After his last breakup, when he'd almost burst into tears at the sight of his weekly Tuesday cocoa, he'd decided that no. He was going to pause the dating until he found someone who made him feel as warm and safe as Warren did.

He was still paused.

But it was Tuesday morning, and no matter how cold and frosty it was outside, or how cold and empty his bed was, Georgie would get to feel the warmth of grumpy affection for a few moments at least.

The car park was icy when he pulled in, carefully avoiding any black ice, but he still almost skipped across the lot to the back door for loading.

Or at least, he would have done if Kacie Wade hadn't turned into the parking lot, skidded on a patch of ice, and almost crashed into him.

There are those moments when the whole world slows down to a crawl, and this was one of them. Georgie heard the car before he saw it, and then all he could hear was the sluggish sound of his heartbeat in his ears as he backed away from the oncoming vehicle, slipped and fell backwards, banging his head against the frame of the door.

"Georgie?! Georgie?!"

When he blearily opened his eyes, Kacie was hovering above him, the accountant clearly shaken.

"Hey Kacie," his words were slow and slightly slurred. "Are you okay? That looked pretty scary."

There was a gruff, curt laugh from next to him, but when he went to turn his head to look, a short "Don't even think about it, Georgie," put a stop to his movements.

"Am I okay?! I'm fine!" Kacie was jittery in a way that Georgie had never seen before. Her usual tight bun had come undone, and her suit jacket was hanging open. "You hit your head, Georgie! Oh Warren, is he going to be okay?"

And then that gruff calm voice again, from right beside Georgie's ear. "He'll likely be fine Kacie, but could you get the door please? I want to get him inside."

Georgie's attempts to stand were more than a little Bambi-like, so Warren did the one thing he never really did, and that was touch Georgie.

And boy was it a touch.

He literally scooped up Georgie, one arm under his knees, and the other behind his shoulders, and carried him into Stuffie Hospital as if Georgie weighed no more than a feather.

His heartbeat seemed to right itself and, giving into temptation, Georgie just curled up into Warren. He didn't even look up at where he knew that salt and pepper beard would be focused straight ahead. Just snuggled up nice and warm and as he rested his head against Warren's chest, he heard the other man's heartbeat, going at quite the pace.

"Your heart's going very fast Warren, are you okay?"

"Boy, I swear if you don't start worrying about yourself, instead of asking after everyone else..." There was a loud huff and then, more gently, "You gave me a shock, Georgie-boy. I'm worried that you might have a concussion, and I want to get you checked out as quickly as possible."

"Oh."

Georgie lapsed into silence as Warren took him into an

office off the stockroom that Georgie had never seen inside before. There was a bed, and a desk, and a first aid poster on the wall.

"Stuffie Hospital has its own first aid room?"

"We like to look after people as well as stuffies."

Warren set him down so gently, Georgie barely felt the mattress coming up to meet him. "I can get up—"

"You can sit down whilst I get you an ice pack. And once I've confirmed that we don't need to take you to hospital, then you can call and reschedule your appointments."

"But—" The look Warren gave him when those broad shoulders turned, probably should have made Georgie feel chastised. Instead, he felt the distinct urge to giggle. Strict Warren was even gruffer than usual and he was all big and grumpy and *nice*. So so nice to look after Georgie like this, and he was clearly focusing very hard on looking after him.

It was sweet, and the kind of thing he'd come to expect from the other man, but it didn't change the fact that it made Georgie wonder who was looking after *him*.

"I can't reschedule the appointments; it's my last day of deliveries so people can make the final tweaks to items before sending them off for Christmas." He turned big wide eyes on Warren, and was satisfied to note that the other man's Adam's apple bobbed once. Twice. "I can't let down my clients before Christmas."

"Fine. I'll do the deliveries. But you are to *stay here*, and Kacie is going to sit with you."

Kacie popped her head round the doorframe, clearly having hovered outside and smiled shyly. "As long as that's okay with you, Georgie?"

Georgie nodded and then winced as his head throbbed. "Yeah, that's fine with me."

Warren sat on the chair besides the bed and leaned in to

place an icepack behind Georgie's head. "There you; can you hold that in place for me please?"

"Yes Sir." The words were jokey, but as soon as they left Georgie's lips, he felt like the ground was going to swallow him up. He dropped his eyes and would have shuffled away, best he could, if Warren hadn't taken Georgie's chin in his hand, and nudged it up until their eyes met.

Warren's eyes were the kind of bright blue that belongs to a sky on a hot summer's day. They felt oddly out of place in the middle of winter, like they'd warm up anyone who saw them. And they warmed Georgie now.

"I was only—"

"Georgie boy," Warren dropped his voice so Kacie couldn't hear. "If you want to call me Sir, that's fine by me, but I really think that's a conversation for when I know that you aren't half concussed. Now, where's your phone? I would like you to have my number in case of emergencies."

And all whilst Warren was putting his number into Georgie's phone, and talking through care and checks with Kacie, all Georgie could think was *But I don't want to call you Sir. I want to call you Daddy...*

10

All afternoon, Georgie had visitor after visitor to the first aid room. Ralphie and Lillie came bounding in as soon as they heard about the accident, and even Ms Owens, who owned Stuffie Hospital, came to check on him and asked him if he was okay.

And all the while, Kacie sat by his bed, typing furiously on her laptop.

"What're you working on?" he asked her, during a momentary lull in conversation.

"The accounts, she said, flashing a spreadsheet at him. "Speaking of which…Warren puts in a lot of orders to you."

"Yeah?"

"More than he's done to any other supplier."

Georgie felt himself flush under her gaze. "I—"

She grinned suddenly, and the professional veneer that came over her every time any member of the Stuffie Hospital team entered the room vanished. "It's okay. It's really kind of sweet. But also, he must really value you as a colleague; he wouldn't do that just because he likes you."

Georgie fought the urge to bounce on the bed. He tried

an experimental wriggle and the abandoned it when he realised that it didn't help his head. "You think he likes me?"

She looked at him, slightly confused. "Georgie, he *carried* you into the building."

"Yes, but he's lovely; he'd do that for anyone."

"Lillie wasn't very well a few weeks ago. He looked after her, but he didn't carry her anywhere."

It took a moment to process that. Just like it had when Warren had said that it'd be fine if he called him Sir. Huh. Maybe, whilst all this time he'd been holding up every man he met against what he'd called the Warren Scale, he should actually just have turned to Warren himself.

"Plus—" She was quiet suddenly.

"Kacie?"

"He calls you 'Georgie boy'." There was a longing in her eyes that made Georgie want to reach over and hug her until that hurt went away. "That's kind of a special thing." He noticed her fiddling then, with the tiny lion on her keychain. "You shouldn't ignore that, I don't think."

It was somewhat strange to have this woman, usually so composed and put together, share a moment of vulnerability with him.

"I've never really been Georgie boy before," he admitted. "I have had boyfriends, but they weren't like Warren. They were..." His voice trailed off and it wasn't until his fingernails bit into his palm that he realised he'd been clenching his fists.

That quiet nod of acknowledgement from Kacie, made him feel like he could continue. "I was always too loud, too bouncy, too enthusiastic. Almost as if they wanted a toy to sit in the corner silently, that they could take out and play with sometimes. Not that," he chuckled, the sound harsh in the quiet between them, "being a toy is necessarily a bad thing. I just—"

"Just not like that." Kacie's eyes glinted with unshed tears, and impulsively she reached out and took his hand in hers. "You deserve the chance to be someone's Georgie boy. We all deserve chances like that."

And then her hand was gone and she was standing up, straightening her skirt and redoing her bun. "I'd best leave you to the ministrations of our first aider then," and Georgie realised that Warren had been standing in the doorway for some time, at least.

"Did you hear all of that?"

Warren nodded just the once, and came to take the seat that Kacie had just vacated. "You know that you're not a toy to me, right? I like that you've business savvy, and are funny and kind. And I like that you make my Tuesdays a little bit brighter, louder, and bouncy. Those are part of what make you you, and no one should ever make you feel like you have to change any of that."

Georgie met his gaze, head on. "Yes, but people always say that. They just don't realise that they don't mean it until after they've gotten to know me better."

Warren ran his hand across the bristles of his beard, and was quiet for a long time. "I suppose you might have a point in that we don't know each other as much as I'd like to. I'm fairly convinced that you don't have concussion, but I'd still like to keep an eye on you, just in case. How about you stay in my guest bedroom tonight, and you can see for yourself that you don't bother me in the slightest?"

That was a suggestion. And one that made Georgie feel all kinds of squirmy.

"Besides," continued Warren, you don't know that my not speaking too much wouldn't annoy you."

"Oh no!" said Georgie, impulsively, "I've always wanted a Daddy who was strong and silent. They feel safer."

There was a pause, and he realised what he'd said, but

before he could hide his face in his pillow, Warren was talking again, talking more than Georgie had ever heard him talk before. "Now, I'm not always silent, but I understand what you mean. And I've always wanted a Little boy who'd bring me out of my shell a bit."

"We don't have to…"

"No, we don't."

"And I could just spend time with you?"

"Of course. And my spare room is very cosy."

"Okay then." Georgie nodded and was rewarded with a smile that was sunnier than the days Warren's eyes made him think of.

After Warren's work day finished, he drove Georgie back to Georgie's place, so he could pick up a couple of bits and pieces for the night. He hadn't, however, been prepared for the sheer magic of Georgie's flat.

Georgie had always liked Christmas. His parents hadn't been great at celebrating it, or indeed great at much in general, but his grandmother had always allowed him to help her decorate her house, and when she died, she left him all of her decorations. Her house hadn't been very big, but it had definitely been bigger than Georgie's place, and there wasn't really space for all of her decorations.

He made space.

Every surface was covered in figurines or ornaments, there were no less than three Christmas trees, each with their own colour scheme, and there was tinsel *everywhere*.

It was, he realised as he watched Warren take it all in, quite a lot.

"You like Christmas then?"

Georgie's peal of laughter made them both relax a little. "Yeah, I like Christmas."

"I haven't put my decorations up yet; I don't suppose you'd like to—"

"*Yes!*" His enthusiasm was obvious. "Okay, I'll grab my things, and then we can get going."

It was fairly easy to grab the things he'd need for an overnight stay from his bedroom—washbag; pyjamas; clothes for the following day—and then he stopped and looked at Blitzen.

Blitzen had been one of those impulsive purchases that he probably should have regretted, what with his price, but he definitely didn't. He also wasn't solely a Christmas stuffie either, though that was in part due to the fact that Georgie didn't think that he actually had anywhere big enough to put him when the festive season ended.

He slung his bag over his shoulder and grabbed Blitzen – arms barely reaching around the reindeer stuffie's waist— before stumbling with him back into the living room.

He wasn't entirely certain what Warren's reaction would be to seeing a stuffie that was literally as tall as Georgie was, but he wasn't disappointed. There was a widening of eyes and then a deep laugh that he'd never heard before.

Oh. That was unexpected.

Warren sat down heavily on the sofa, narrowly avoiding tinsel falling on his head, and just leaned back and belly laughed. "If I was still wondering about you being a Little, after that Daddy comment earlier, *that* has put aside any questions."

"I'm sure I don't know what you're talking about," but it was hard to be taken seriously when poking your head between two antlers to speak.

"Sure you don't; come on Georgie boy, I'll give you a hand."

And watching Warren carry Blitzen down the stairs to the car was actually the sweetest feeling. He genuinely didn't care about how he looked, or that a giant reindeer was going to invade his place. What he cared about was that Georgie wanted to bring his reindeer stuffie with him, and therefore Warren would bring the reindeer stuffie.

It was a nice feeling.

The kind of feeling that Georgie always felt that a Daddy Dom should make him feel.

And then when they arrived at Warren's house, the first thing Warren did was find a spot for Blitzen to sit in. "Come on in you, and get cosy whilst I go dig out my decorations."

Left alone in the room, Georgie spun on the spot for a moment. It was very…Warren. Lots of wood and dark browns and an open fireplace. Solid.

Georgie wanted solid in his life.

Needed solid in his life.

Someone other than just Blitzen to cuddle at night.

And someone who'd put up Christmas decorations, just because Georgie liked Christmas.

11

As they put up Christmas decorations, Georgie taking point and deciding where things would go (aside from some very sadly, straggly tinsel that should have been put out of its misery years ago), he kept catching Warren smiling at him.

Finally, he turned around hands, on his hips and looked at Warren, one eyebrow quirked in a fashion that Georgie considered to be more than a little debonair. "Why do you keep smiling at me?"

"Because you're all kinds of lovely when you're excited."

That made him blink. "Oh. I mean, sure, of course I am."

Warren laughed, and reached over to straighten a Christmas bauble. "It's been years since I put any of this stuff up. Not because I'm a scrooge, or even because I don't celebrate, but more because there doesn't seem to be much point when it's just me here."

"That seems sad." Georgie walked over, and cautiously slipped his hand into the other man's. "Will it be difficult having them up after I've gone?"

Warren turned away and there was a stab of rejection that Georgie pushed down pretty hard. He wasn't being rejected right now; he probably just needed space.

There was a mumble that came from Warren's back, and Georgie had to ask for clarification. "Sorry?"

"I was hoping that maybe you'd come back and see them again?"

Oh. *Oh.*

His gruff friend was shy. Well, wasn't that just utterly adorable?!

He bounded up, and hip checked Warren vigorously. "I'd love that. In what capacity?"

"Capacity?"

Gently, he took Warren's hands in his and tugged him until they stood face to face. "Kacie thinks you might like me."

Warren looked around at all of the Christmas decorations, and then more pointedly at Blitzen in the corner. "Do you doubt her word?"

"No, I'm beginning to think that she might be right."

"Good," and then Warren was slipping his fingers in the belt loops of Georgie's jeans and tugged him even closer. "She is right."

From here, Georgie could have counted each individual eyelash that framed those blue eyes. "Well, if she's right…" Fuck those eyes were stunning. "…why haven't you ever done anything about it?"

"I didn't know you wanted me to." Warren's words were a caress, a low rumbly sound that Georgie felt all the way down his toes—and in other places besides.

Okay. So he was going to have to be blunt. "I want you to."

"Yeah?"

Now it was almost frustrating. "Just kiss me, for fuck's sake."

And then Warren's mouth was on his, hard and hot and damn he'd forgotten how much he loved the feel of a beard against his skin, the hairs almost sandpapery in that delicious manner that made his knees go weak.

He fisted his hand in Warren's short hair and was satisfied to hear what he was convinced was an actual *growl* issue from that throat. And then Warren was tearing his mouth away and burying it at that point on Georgie's nape that made him actually cry out. "Fuck!"

Then there was dizzying space that made him reach out to Warren to stabilise him. "Where'd you go?"

"I'm right here Georgie boy, but I'd feel better if you'd had a good night's sleep before we...well, you know?"

"Do I?" Georgie had never really had a predilection for bratting before, but he wanted muss up all that tightly controlled Warren-ness until he took exactly what he wanted. Namely Georgie.

"Fine, you want it that way? I want to know that you're fine and rested and without the slightest trace of concussion before I fuck your brains out."

Georgie's brain short-circuited.

Those words worked. They *definitely* worked. And when he spoke in reply, it wasn't even really a word, more of an outbreath dressed up as an *oh.*

"So, what do we do now?"

"Now we curl up under a blanket on the couch, and watch your favourite Christmas movie, and eat all of the snacks you want."

That had Georgie's attention for sure, and without even thinking about it, he was Little. A ball of excited, festive energy, bouncing on the balls of his feet until Warren pressed a gently kiss to his temple. "Yes please please please please please."

His movie of choice was an animated affair about a member of Santa's family who just wanted to prove himself, and it was sweet and funny and Warren laughed in all of the right places, and then in some other places when Georgie got enthusiastic about his favourite bits.

But it wasn't a horrible kind of laugh, like some of Georgie's exes. It had sometimes felt with them that they were pointing and laughing at Georgie, treating him like some kind of freak for their amusement. Whereas Warren laughed in delight: delight in Georgie's enthusiasm; delight in Georgie's happiness; and delight in Georgie.

And each rumbly laugh made Georgie feel that little bit safe. Like it was a blanket being wrapped tightly around him.

They paused the film for food—mini sausage rolls, pineapple and cheese on sticks, crisps; all the best party food —and then when they settled back down to continue watching, there was some definite snuggling.

It was hard to snuggle with other people sometimes, especially if they had long limbs which poked you, but this kind of snuggling was perfect. Just gathered up, and sat on Warren's lap, arms around him, holding him tight, and that rumbly laugh making both of them shake.

Georgie felt it. That *thing* that he'd always wanted.

He was so comfortable, that it had seemed perfectly natural and say "Daddy, can I have some hot chocolate," without even thinking.

And Warren had said "Of course Georgie boy," as if he'd been Georgie's Daddy always. Though the more Georgie thought about it, the more he realised that Warren kind of *had* been Daddy-like with him.

He always made him hot chocolate; he listened to his

excitable chattering; and he always made him feel safe and cared for.

Huh.

Georgie had a Daddy.

But when it was time for bed, he almost started whining at the thought of being in the spare room. "But I want more *cuddles,*" he said, not caring how needy it made him sound.

Warren moved Georgie off his lap and next to him on the coach. "Okay, I need you to be big for a moment here Georgie."

Georgie rolled his eyes, stuck his tongue out, and then quickly straightened up when he got a Look from Warren. "Okay, okay." One deep breath, and then two, and then he was back. "I'm big now."

He sounded disappointed, even to himself, and Warren must have picked up on his tone, because he said sharply, "Big Georgie is just as welcome here as Little Georgie, and I can't talk negotiations with you when you're in Littlespace. It just wouldn't be fair."

Warren was right, Georgie knew that, but it still sucked. Littlespace was fun and safe and Little Georgie didn't usually care if other people weren't being too nice to him. Big Georgie cared a lot. "I know."

"Right, so."

And this was it. This was the moment when Warren was going to tell him that it had been fun for an evening, but he really didn't want Little Georgie long term.

"I need to check where you're at. And we should establish safewords. Just in case Little Georgie needs a break in a scene. Or if Big Georgie wants to stop something."

"So you're not stopping this?"

"Stopping—Georgie, surely you can see how much I care for you. How much I have *always* cared for you. My living room looks like a fucking winter wonderland." It did look like a winter wonderland. They'd done an excellent job. "I definitely don't want to stop, unless you do?"

"No!" The word came out louder than Georgie expected, and he repeated it, more quietly. "No, I don't want to stop. I just thought that maybe I was being too whiny."

"Oh," Warren suddenly understood and leaned forward and gave Georgie the gentlest kiss. "No, I don't mind that your Little is feeling whiny and clingy. It's understandable after a very long day. I just want to check in and see what you need before we go to sleep."

It was all a little bit too much; to know that not only was he wanted, but that he was wanted just as he was, in all the many versions of Georgie. He started to cry and Warren swept him up in his arms and just held him as sobs racked Georgie's body.

And it wasn't cute crying either. No this was whole body sobbing that made his nose run and tinged his eyes with red. Gross.

But that didn't stop Warren from picking him up and carrying him into the bedroom.

The covers that he tucked Georgie under were grey and plain, but they were warm and comforting, and when he returned with a big bottle of water, Warren insisted Georgie drink most of it before he was allowed to lie back down.

"Crying can dehydrate you, and I don't want my boy getting dehydrated."

"Yes, Daddy," mumbled Georgie, and then tried to burrow under the covers until he could get as close as possible to Warren.

"Right, before bed, check in please."

Georgie nodded.

"Are you okay?"

"Yes, just tired and sleepy and," he snuck a cheeky look at the other man, "feeling snuggly."

That rumbly laugh again and then, "And your safeword?"

"Christmas."

This time laughter was more of a shout than a rumble. "Christmas it is. Now come here boy, and let me hold you."

And for the first time in a long time, Georgie fell asleep in someone's arms.

School 12 School

Georgie woke up with an insistent erection.

It wasn't his fault; he couldn't help it if being wrapped in the arms of a bearded gruff Daddy like Warren made him melt and want to hump in equal measure.

"Mmmmmm." Warren leaned round to pull him back in close and oh. Goodness. Turns out Warren had an insistent erection as well; or at least it certainly felt that way.

Georgie did an experimental wiggle and was gratified to hear the curse that emanated from the man behind him, and then there was some shifting and quick movements and oh good grief Warren was above him, growling in that rumbly gruff way that made Georgie want to be eaten all the way up.

"Wiggles, Georgie? Really?"

"I was wondering what reaction they'd get."

Warren stopped bracing above Georgie long enough for Georgie to feel his hard cock against his thigh. It didn't matter that they were both pyjama-ed, that was definitely a hard cock.

He squeaked and damn if Warren's face didn't become wolfish.

"That's a…a whole reaction."

"Isn't it." Warren leaned in and kissed him, and Georgie kissed him back eagerly, wrapping his arms around Warren's neck to pull him in tighter, so he could hump his leg a little. "Morning Georgie, how are you today?"

"Well, I'm just waiting for that fucking you promised me." His mischievous look met one of hunger and then he was gasping and moaning as his gruff Daddy bit down on his shoulder.

"You think you can tell *me* what to do?"

"Ummm…" Georgie reached down cautiously and brushed his hand against where Warren's cock was straining in his pyjama bottoms. "Yeah, I think so."

Another bite and Georgie closed his eyes so hard he saw stars behind his eyelids. Fuck that was good, the biting and then the sucking and then the flickering of a tongue against his skin and *fuuuuuuuck.*

Warren lifted his head, breathing jagged, and he nudged at Georgie, until Georgie opened his eyes again. "What's your safeword?"

"Huh?"

"Your safeword Georgie, what's your safeword?"

"Oh, Christmas. It's Christmas, Daddy."

That made them both grin and they were still laughing when Warren rolled them over until Georgie was sitting astride his lap.

"So, tell me, Georgie boy, what is it that you want for Christmas?"

"Cock please!" It sounded jokey, but they both heard the truth in his words, and undercurrent of desperation that had Warren reaching out and popping buttons off Georgie's shirt as he ripped open.

"I'll sew the buttons back on myself, but right now I'd like you naked for me."

Georgie wasn't sure if he'd ever stripped faster. It was intoxicating, being consumed by a gaze that was unwavering. Made the whole experience that much hotter, and then when he stepped out of his pyjama bottoms, Warren leaned across the bed, half hanging off, to wrap his hand around Georgie's dick.

He was surprised he didn't come on the spot.

"I don't think," Warren's words were barely restrained, "that I've ever wanted anyone so badly. Each time you come flitting into my office and drink your hot chocolate with those big eyes, and dance around without ever even touching me... Each time it's all I can do not to take you in my arms and kiss you until you melt for me."

"Yes please." Georgie's voice was trembling now, and he was rewarded with a few quick jerks, before being hauled back onto the bed.

And then it was Warren's turn to get undressed, and if Georgie could have caught and captured every single second of that undressing, he would have. Silvery hair leading down to a cock that was neither too large, nor too small. Just perfect for a Christmas dicking.

He lay backwards, his legs hitched up so that he was displayed lewdly to Warren's gaze, and there was a dizzying moment of fingers and lube, which made Georgie arch up off the bed, muttering curses and pleading all at once. One, two and then three digits filling him until he could barely breathe.

The tearing of a condom wrapper and then Warren was leaning over Georgie, kissing him gently. "What time of year is it Georgie boy?"

That was his opportunity to safeword, if all this was too much, but all he said, with a smirk on his face, was "time for the festive stuffing," and then Warren was laughing, that rumbly laugh, as he slowly inched his cock into Georgie's lubed arse.

He was pretty pleased with that stuffing joke, but any other holiday puns flew out of his head as he adjusted to the size of Warren, stretching his arse, and then sliding in, deeper and deeper until his cock hit Georgie's prostate and fuck fuck fuck. Yes. Just there. Please.

Georgie was babbling, he was sure, legs up, arse filled, but then his words disappeared completely, stolen by the rumbly growl that crept across his skin. He felt like he was being devoured by Warren, caught up by this hunger that consumed them both, and the rumbles set is skin aflame.

And it was almost too intense to bear, the pressure building, until his name, strangled flew from Warren's voice and then they were moving together, against each other, faster and faster until he was coming.

With a gasp, Warren followed and fell about Georgie's neck, and Georgie found himself petting his Daddy's head, scattering kisses across his brow as they both gasped for air. It was nice, in this moment, to show Warren as much care as he'd shown Georgie. Kisses, stolen brief touches, and then more passionate, before Warren got up to dispose of the condom, and get a damp flannel to clean up Georgie. He did so with gentle strokes, interspersed with kisses, until they were both clean, and then bundled up together, back under the covers.

"That was nice, Daddy," said Georgie, wrapped up in his arms.

"It was better than nice Georgie boy, it was perfect."

That made him smile and he wiggled happily. "Daddy…?"

"Yes?"

"Do *you* like Christmas?"

"I like how happy it makes you."

That was a sweet answer, but Georgie couldn't shake the

feeling that all those Christmas decorations in a big house on his own would result in a sad Daddy come Christmas Day. "Well, I get extra happy on Christmas Day." He shuffled round and leaned up to kiss Warren's lips. "Want to see how happy I get on Christmas Day?"

Happy gruff rumbles and more kisses assured him that yes, Warren most definitely would.

"And what should I bring my Georgie boy for Christmas."

"Why," said Georgie, curled up in his Daddy's arms, "I already got the best gift ever. My very own gruff Daddy for Christmas."

A LITTLE'S TURTLE

ELLIE ROSE

✣ 13 ✣

That didn't sound good.

Walking past the Great Wall of Stuffies, Bobbie Sanders paused to listen.

The pipes in the Restoration Hub were getting increasingly cranky. She'd already booked in for a plumber to come look at it, as she was more of an electrics gal and general handywoman than pipes and water, and she was hoping beyond hope that it'd hold out until then. Besides, now that it was quiet, she had jobs to do.

As the Stuffie Hospital site manager, she stayed on site until 9pm every Saturday night—which made for an oh so spirited social life. Not. But if she was completely honest, she really didn't care. It meant that once all the hustle and bustle of staff and patients had died down, and gone home for the day, it was just her, her toolbox, and several hundred stuffies to watch over her as she worked through the final things on her weekly to do list.

Her ex had denounced the Great Wall of Stuffies as decidedly creepy, and said that they loomed rather than watched, but there was a reason why the woman was

Bobbie's ex. Same with the guy before that. For some reason they just didn't understand the pure joy that came with working at Stuffie Hospital. Bobbie didn't have to hide her smile around her co-workers; didn't have to pretend to be dismissive of those who came in, clutching a beloved stuffie that needed repairs. It made her week, being surrounded by sunny people, working for a company that worked to bring joy to others – whether through general repairs, or the work that they did with the children's unit at the actual hospital, or the local domestic violence shelter. Repairing stuffies might not seem important, but it was important to those whose lives they touched. And Bobbie got to be a small part of that by keeping the site running as smoothly as possible.

They were closed Sundays and Mondays, so she had two days from tomorrow, in which to chill out and unwind, but Bobbie had a habit of liking things *just so*, and really couldn't relax if she knew she'd left some odd job undone. So here she was, 8pm on a Saturday night, about to go round and make sure that all of the worktables in the Restoration Hub had their joints tightened so they didn't wobble.

She set her toolbox down on Lillie's station and opened it up.

An adorable turtle stuffie smiled shyly up at her out of it, his green head stalwartly cheerful despite the odd streak of oil across his shell. She patted him absentmindedly on the head whilst grabbing her screwdriver.

Everyone knew that Bobbie had a soft spot for the stuffies, but it had been the business' finance manager, Kacie Wade, who'd walked into Bobbie's office with Turtle, popped him on her desk, and walked out without a single comment. When she'd tried to talk to the woman about why, Kacie said in a very no-nonsense tone that she was fed up of seeing Bobbie look longingly at the Great Wall, and needed one of her own. The words sounded harsh, but there was a twinkle in her eye, and a tiny lion stuffie on her keychain that made Bobbie wonder if Kacie knew more about wanting stuffies than she let on.

Either way, Turtle had become a permanent fixture in her toolbox. He'd gotten a little greasy, and she was fairly certain that his oil streaks were now permanent fixtures, but that didn't mean that he was any less loved.

But as she tightened the screws at Lillie's workstation, Bobbie tried very hard not to think about what had happened when her ex had seen Turtle in her toolbox.

Perhaps some small part of her had known that Dana wouldn't like it, which is why she'd hidden Turtle in her work toolbox, but inevitably she'd forgotten one day, doing a job in her flat, as his little head peeked out of the top. There'd been some shouting and throwing around of words like 'freak' and 'weirdo', and it had been all Bobbie could do not to curl up in a ball on the floor and cry.

In fact, she'd done exactly that when her ex left, lifting Turtle out of her toolbox, sat on the floor and rocking back and forth on the spot. The softness of his fur beneath her fingers soothed her a little, and she'd sat there for over an hour, cheeks tear-stained and her thumb in her mouth.

That night she did everything she'd ever wanted to do that her ex had dismissed out of hand. She made herself a pillow fort on her living room floor and stayed up watching cartoons, and ate so much ice cream she almost felt sick. She wrapped blankets around her until she was almost cocooned, and let herself play with Turtle and cuddle Turtle and cry with Turtle.

But Bobbie had only allowed herself that one night of weakness. The next day she'd blocked her ex on all social media, put a box marked 'Dana' outside her apartment door for the other woman to pick up, and thrown herself into work with a ferocity that the rest of the Stuffie Hospital team wisely chose not to comment on, even if she did find more cookies and cups of coffee on her desk than usual. Everyone knew something was up, even if they didn't ask her why.

And Turtle returned to her toolbox and stayed there.

Maybe it was then that she'd stopped allowing people to look after her, although that wasn't quite true, she'd never really allowed anyone to look after her. Not as a kid, not in foster care, not after. The only person who'd ever looked out for Bobbie was Abi, the owner of Stuffie Hospital, and Bobbie was fairly certain that the only reason she accepted that was because they'd both been foster kids, though at different times. Dana hadn't looked after her, and the ex before her *certainly* hadn't looked after Bobbie. They'd demanded time and energy and never gave much of their own in return. Perhaps that's why those relationships hadn't lasted, or perhaps it was because Bobbie really wanted someone to consider her a little more. To care for her.

No. She didn't need people to care for her, that was *her* job. It was her job to make sure that everything in Stuffie Hospital was safe for those who came through its doors every day. That was how she cared for them. So, Bobbie worked and worked and then spent her days off sleeping and playing video games starring an Italian plumber and a green turtle not too dissimilar to her own Turtle.

Joints on the workstation tightened, she straightened up and rolled her eyes as the pipes started rumbling again. "Hush," she said, looking sternly in the direction of the pipe elbow that seemed to be the most offending culprit.

Unfortunately, the elbow seemed not to heed her words, and she was just about to walk over and have a tentative look at the scenario, when *something* happened to the threads connecting the elbow to the piping either end, and a jet of water hit her squarely in the face.

14

By the time the emergency plumber arrived, Bobbie was a mess.

First, she'd tried to use her wrench to tighten the pipe threads. That had been a fucking disaster; they'd ended up coming out completely and then the water was *everywhere.*

She'd then spent half an hour using towels, rags, anything she had to hand, to try and stop the water from gushing out of the pipes, before abandoning the attempt in favour of covering workstations in sheets of tarpaulin, to try and stop the tools from being ruined – she'd never been more grateful that most of the fabrics and materials for repairs were kept in a separate stock cupboard – and rescuing the Great Wall of Stuffies.

There had to be over two hundred stuffies in that wall, from teeny little bunnies, to mahoosive bears, and she'd ran back and forth, back and forth, carrying them to her office, so they didn't get even more bedraggled and sad than they already were. And she only somewhat succeeded. These stuffies were the donations, the charity bears that had been given to the hospital, and they usually were passed on to children in need once they were patched up and mended, but most of them were pretty fragile as it was, and getting wet had done more damage than Bobbie thought that even the restoration specialists might be able to repair.

It had been pretty heartbreaking.

When the plumber came in, she couldn't even look at him, hidden as she was under a massive pile of stuffies that she was carting in the direction of her office. She waved a hand in the direction of the Restoration Hub, then grabbed at a rogue chubby dinosaur who threatened to topple out of her hands and ran as fast as she could.

Pausing in her office doorway, having thrown the stuffies through in an attempt to stop them all from spilling out of her arms, she took a deep shuddery breath. She was going to have to call her boss.

Abigail Jenkins was everything you could wish for in a boss, and Bobbie knew that she wouldn't be blamed for this turn events – she'd already had a plumber booked to come look at the pipes next week – but letting Abi down was the last thing she wanted to do. Abi had been the one to hire her straight out of high school, to take a chance on some raggedy kid who had too much sass for her own good, and to pay for training so that Bobbie could do what she'd always wanted: work with her hands; get out of the foster system; and make herself a home.

Her parents hadn't been abusive, just…neglectful, and the system hadn't been much better. So, she'd learnt to depend on no-one but herself. Even Abi, who'd been the best of bosses, hadn't ever been able to quite get Bobbie to shake that way of thinking. And the rest of the Stuffie Hospital team were sweet, and they didn't mind how quiet and hyperfocused Bobbie got on any given project, but she wouldn't have asked them for help with anything. It just wasn't in her nature.

But even Bobbie knew her limits, and her limits were plumbing. Gritting her teeth, she dialled Abigail's number.

"Heya Bobbie, you okay?"

"The pipes—" her voice choked off and she had to take a deep breath and try again. "One of the pipes burst Abi. I've managed to cover most of the workstations, and there's a plumber in there now, but the Restoration Hub's a bit of a mess. I'll come in tomorrow and Monday to clear up, so we can reopen on Tuesday as per usual."

"You'll do no such thing." Abigail's words were direct and Bobbie shuffled from foot to foot, fighting back the argument that sat on the tip of her tongue. "Once you've locked up for tonight, you're to go home and take your damn weekend off – I won't hear otherwise. I'll organise for some day workers to come in and clean up."

"Like hell you—I'll organise the day workers."

There was a chuckle on the other end of the phone. "How about we let Kacie organise the day workers: she'll get a better rate than either of us could get; and I'll come in and supervise. You need your days off Bobbie; you work too hard."

There was truth in Abi's words. Bobbie pushed herself so, during the week. She was usually exhausted by the time her days came round.

"Okay," she conceded. And then added, "The Great Wall of Stuffies is in my office. I didn't want them getting all wet and bedraggled."

"Thank you, Bobbie; that was really good of you to do." And there was that ache again, the one that persisted in raising its ugly head whenever someone praised her. Praise just made her feel awkward, like something was missing from her life that she couldn't quite put her finger on.

"Yeah yeah. Needed doing." Her words were brusque, and she knew she was possibly being a bit rude, but Abi knew her, wouldn't take her words amiss. "I'm going to go see what's happening with the plumber, and I'll text you when everything's sorted and I leave."

"Good job Bobbie, and thank you."

She hung up abruptly and stared at the phone a moment. Good job. No, a good job would have been organising the plumber to come out the moment those pipes had started making noises. Waiting this long really wasn't good enough. Not in the slightest.

Taking one last look at the sound mound of stuffies, abandoned on her office floor, she turned and walked back to the Restoration Hub.

The site was a mess when she walked in, but that wasn't what drew her attention. The sound of water splashing had ceased and she took a sigh of relief. And then she saw him.

The emergency plumber was far more good looking than any video game suggested a plumber could be, with dark hair curling over his brow and deep brown eyes that seemed to smile when she looked at him. It was at that moment that Bobbie realised quite how bedraggled she was looking herself. Her hair had been pulled into a high ponytail, but the water from the pipes meant that it was far from jaunty now, and her t-shirt was plastered to her skin in a way that made her grateful for the grubby denim dungarees that she wore over it. She was not looking her best.

"Hi," he said, and his voice had the lilt of an Italian.

Holy fuck. He was an actual Italian plumber.

Bobbie blinked rapidly several times until she realised that he was waiting for her to reply. "Oh, er, hi." Smooth. "I see you fixed the pipe?"

"I've done *a* fix – replaced the elbow and the threads on this joint – but a lot of this piping needs replacing or you're going to have more issues."

She nodded quietly, trying not to stress about when all

this work was going to get done, and how long it was going to take. "Will we have to close?"

He grimaced. "Possibly? It depends on how bad the other joints are. I'd like to have a quick look round now, just to make sure that none of them are going to – how do you say – go bust, but I can come back in normal working hours to do the actual replacements, so you don't have to pay the higher emergency rates."

"That sounds like a plan," she said, and got her phone out to text Abi an update, and then realised that she had almost definitely been rude and strode over with her hand outstretched. "I'm Bobbie, the site manager here."

He took her hand in one that dwarfed hers, calloused fingers grazing against the palm of her hand and she almost squeaked. "Marco."

Bobbie didn't let people touch her very often, let alone encouraged it. A curt handshake was pretty much the extent of her comfort zone, and yet for some reason she let her hand linger in Marco's. "Hi Marco."

Those deep brown eyes had her flushing, but before she could pull away, he turned and grabbed something off the floor. It was Turtle.

The last hour or so had been tough and frustrating and frankly really fucking unnecessary after a long day at work, but none of that had brought Bobbie even close to tears. But seeing Turtle there, water-clogged and covered in even more dirt and grime than usual, she couldn't fight back the tears that sprung into her eyes.

She took him without a word, and practically ran from the room.

Where to go, where to go. Her office was no good; there was no floor space left with the slew of refugee stuffies in there. Maybe the stock cupboard? Or the staffroom?

Standing in the corridor outside the Hub, Bobbie found

herself frozen in place, starting off in one direction and then stopping, and then again and again and again. She was still stood there when Marco came out after her.

"Bobbie? Are you okay?"

No. She was not okay. It had been a shitty night and she was tired and hungry and Turtle was all wet and everything was just so *rubbish*.

She hadn't realised that she'd been speaking out loud until the word 'rubbish' echoed down the corridor and she realised that she'd shouted it. Her hands trembled as she alternated cuddling Turtle close to her and then flinching away because he was so wet. Ugh. It was all too much. Too much. Too—

A finger tentatively tapped her on the shoulder, and when she turned to look at Marco his worried face was so sweet and so kind that she just fell forward into him. And he didn't even hesitate. He wrapped his arms around her and held her whilst she sobbed, gently stroking her hair and whispering soft words in Italian to her.

After a moment she realised that they were moving, him guiding her towards the couch in the reception area, but when she protested that she was too damp to sit on the couch, he sat down and gestured towards his knee.

This time it was her turn not to hesitate. She settled onto his lap and curled up against his chest with a sigh of contentment that she'd never heard herself make before. And then, before she could stop herself, she said, "Thank you, Daddy."

15

Bobbie had never sat up so fast in her life. She was mortified, horrified, wanted to curl up somewhere that most definitely *wasn't* Marco's lap and pretend that this entire day had never happened.

This is what happens, she told herself, *when you let your guard down. This is why you don't lean on other people. It makes you weak.*

But Marco wasn't recoiling from her, or looking at her in disgust. He was smiling kindly, and chucked her under her chin until she met his eyes.

It didn't stop the torrent of panicked words that fell unstoppered from her mouth though. "I'm sorry. I'm so so sorry, I don't know what came over me, I just—"

"Principessa." The term of endearment cut through her babbling and she looked at him incredulously.

"Princess. Really? Me?! Have you *seen* me?" She gestured at her dungarees, as the wet t-shirt, at the sorry bedraggled mess that she'd become.

For the first time since they'd met, she saw Marco's gaze darken with admonishment. "Yes, I have seen you. I am looking at you right now. Tell me, what makes you think that you're not worthy of being a princess?"

She swallowed. "Princesses are delicate little things. They don't work with wrenches and screwdrivers. They wear pretty dresses and… and… and drink tea and shit. I don't like tea."

Marco laughed, a big bark of a sound that should have made Bobbie feel small and insignificant, but it didn't. She pulled a face at him nonetheless. "Princesses throughout history have done more than wear pretty dresses and drink tea. They have been strong, and fought for and protected their people – just like you did with the cuddlies."

"Cuddlies? Oh, you mean the stuffies." She blushed. She hadn't realised that he'd seen how many of them she'd moved into her office.

"Esattamente. Exactly. Now, principessa, you are not the first Little one to call me Daddy, and I am far from shocked. But I would like to know if you are alright, and truthfully please."

For a moment it was almost too overwhelming, the feeling of relief that swept over her. In that instance of calling him Daddy, she'd been thrown back to Dana hating Turtle, hating *her*, and she couldn't bear to see that look in anyone's eyes ever again. She wanted to bury her head in his chest and not have to look up and face the real world any time soon. The real world was boring and meant responsibilities and having to do everything for herself all of the time.

But he'd asked if she was okay, and she had sobbed all over him, so she should probably answer that at least. "I'm…" she paused, wanting to be as truthful as he'd requested. "I'm feeling a bit wobbly. The pipes were stressful enough, but Turtle," and here she offered him up for perusal, "Turtle is super special to me. And seeing him all wet and dirty was really upsetting." She dropped her eyes and bit her lip.

It was happening now, that feeling that came over her when she went Little. The shyness and the need to please and be praised. She tried to push it down, but his impulsive hug made all her vulnerability come flooding back up.

"I'm really proud of you, principessa. You did really well, telling me how you're feeling. Now, are you going to be okay here whilst I get you some water, and then finish checking the pipes?"

Bobbie nodded and barely even whimpered when he carefully disentangled her and placed her on the couch. His absence was fleeting, and then he was back with a glass of water and a blanket that he'd rustled up from somewhere – probably from behind the reception desk – and pressed her phone into her hand and told her to call someone whilst he worked.

She baulked at that, especially when he made her take a photo of his id and send it to her boss. But he stood over her, tapping his foot until she finally gave in and called Abi.

"Hi Abi."

"Are you okay Bobbie?"

She stuck her tongue out Marco and he grinned and ruffled her hair before heading back towards the Restoration Hub. "The pipes are all fixed and Marco is going to check that there aren't any urgent issues. And then he'll come back and fix the bits that need fixing. It's going to cost money and also time – we'll probably have to close the Hub for maybe a week. Possibly elsewhere too."

There was a pause on the other end of the phone, and then Abi said, "Bobbie, you sound a little bit different."

"Rude!" she knew that she was sounding bratty now, but she couldn't help herself. "A little bit different indeed."

"Bobbie, are you able to look after yourself right now?"

Bobbie stuck her tongue out, and then realised that her boss couldn't see the action down the phone. "That's not fair. You can't say stuff like that, just because you're my boss. I'm fine. I'm more than capable of looking after myself."

"I can if I'm worried about you." Those words gave her pause.

"I'm okay. Marco's looking after me. He made me send you his id."

Another pause whilst Abi clearly went searching for the photo. "*Ohhhhhhhh.*"

"What?!"

This time when she spoke, Bobbie could hear amusement bubbling over in Abi's voice. "I know Marco, we have some… mutual friends. He's a good sort. Can I speak to him?"

Bobbie wanted to refuse, but out of everyone in her life, Abi was probably the only one whom she'd let get even slightly close, and that was only because she'd once been in the foster system too. There was something about that kind of experience, that unspoken knowledge, which meant that she trusted the older woman. Somewhat.

"Marco?" she called.

"Si, principessa?" He came running, and she allowed herself a moment of admiring him, before thrusting the phone in his direction.

"Abi wants to speak to you!"

He took the phone, and no matter how hard she tried, she couldn't quite hear what Abi was saying on the other end of the phone.

When he handed it back to her, she almost leant into his smile, before remembering that her boss was on the other end of the line.

"I've spoken to Marco, and his shift finishes after this, so he's going to take you home."

"I can get the bus."

The chorus of nos, from both Abi and Marco made her grin.

"It's true though! I always get the bus home after work."

A string of Italian words emanated from Marco that Bobbie couldn't understand, but when she looked at him questioningly, he stopped his muttering and just shook his head. "I will take you home principessa."

She rolled her eyes at him. "Fine."

"And text me when you're home safe please," said Abi.

"*Fine.*"

"And have fun."

Fun? What could Abi mean?

arco had one of those trucks that you had to practically haul yourself up into, and he was bemused when Bobbie insisted on clambering up all on her own. She knew, because he'd laughed and almost kissed her when he leant over her to click her seatbelt into place.

She'd looked at him, daring him to kiss her and he only grinned and gently pressed the back of his hand against her cheek before jumping down and closing the door to the passenger seat.

This was fun. Or rather, it would have been if her clothes had dried out, but they were still slightly damp, and Bobbie couldn't help but keep wriggling in her seat.

"You okay, mia principessa?"

She heard the 'my', the 'mia', this time and tried very hard not to beam. "Yes, thank you, Daddy!"

This time her use of the honorific was deliberate, a testing of the water, and she held her breath to see what his reaction would be.

Leaning in, he nudged her nose with his, and then leaned

back. "We need to have a conversation about you calling me Daddy, Little one."

She wrinkled her nose. "You don't like it?"

"I like it a lot, but you need to make that decision when you're not feeling quite so Little and so overwhelmed."

That made sense. Bobbie didn't know why her very logical, always in charge, brain hadn't suggested this already. Oh. Because she was Little of course. "That makes sense I s'pose." She sighed. "What should I call you tonight then?"

"Marco is fine, and I can just call you Bobbie instead of principessa, if you like."

That was a difficult one, because she really wasn't very princess-y, but when Marco called her principessa she felt all melty and wobbly and Little. "You may call me principessa," she said imperiously, and deigned not to notice when he laughed at her. Mainly because it felt like he was laughing with her.

When he pulled up outside her place, she barely hesitated before asking him in.

"Principessa, you gotta be careful. You can't just invite anyone into your home."

"It's okay," she said, grinning at him, "Abi said she knows you, and she'd hunt you down if you hurt me."

"She would?"

"Of course! And I'd do the same for her!" Her words were unfiltered, the way her thoughts often felt when she was Little, but Bobbie realised that they were true. She might not be the kind of person to wax lyrical about another, but she really would do almost anything for Abi. And her boss would do the same. "I'm going to text her and let her know you're coming in for coffee."

Marco made a noise and she looked at him curiously. "Maybe just un po'd'acqua, some water. It's a bit late for coffee and besides, the coffee here is..." his voice trailed off and he made a face. "Anyway, it's far too late for principessas to be drinking coffee; you'd never get to sleep!"

She muttered something under her voice about video games and he looked vaguely horrified. "Mia principessa, you'd stay up playing video games all night?"

"It's a Saturday," she protested, "I don't have work until Tuesday! Usually, I spend my days off sleeping and gaming. It's cosy. And relaxing."

"Hmph." His little huff was kind of adorable, and she felt herself wanting to nudge him some more until she got him to do it again and again. Very cute indeed.

But he followed her down the path to her ground floor townhouse apartment.

It was definitely cosy. Dana had called it cramped, but Bobbie loved her home. She'd saved every cent she could, those first eight years working at Stuffie Hospital, and Abi had co-signed her mortgage application – she didn't think it would've been approved without that. But no one would be able to drag her away from the stability those four walls offered. This was her own space, her own home, and she had more safety and security here than she'd had at any other point in her life.

No one could take this away.

She snuck a look at Marco as he followed her in, but he just looked about and smiled, like he could see why this was hers.

You walked straight into her kitchen, which she'd always liked, as it felt warm and welcoming, and then that opened onto her living room, with her bed tucked around the corner. She even had a bath as well as a shower – which felt very decadent for a humble studio apartment.

And it wasn't fussy or ornate. Simple colours, greens and creams, and plants doted around almost every surface, making up for the lack of a garden.

It was a calm space.

"I like it," he said, "It feels like you," and she'd practically glowed at that. Not everyone understood her. Most people assumed that her job and the way she dressed meant she felt masc, and that her soft, warm apartment didn't fit with her. Which wasn't fair, because she was soft and warm, she just didn't let most people show it.

But somehow, in one evening, Marco had seen it.

She blamed Turtle.

She was still holding the stuffie, and she popped into the bathroom, and set up dish soap in the sink the way that she'd seen Lillie and Rebecca do at work, and popped Turtle in to soak. And then popped a kiss on the top of his head, because it wasn't really his fault.

Marco was sitting on a stool by her breakfast bar when she came back in. He had his back to her and was looking at one of her plants, stroking its leaves, and she didn't say anything for a moment. Just watched. He wasn't particularly broad, but there was a strength in his shoulders that spoke of more than just work in construction. Strength that spoke to that protective streak she'd seen when he'd insisted on driving her home.

All of a sudden, Bobbie felt very Big indeed, and when she spoke, her Little voice had retreated. "What would you like to drink, Marco?"

When he looked at her, he saw the change, and nodded, and smiled again. The man seemed to always be smiling. "Perhaps I could put the kettle on whilst you change out of those damp clothes?" She raised an eyebrow and he hurriedly added, "Not like that, just that you didn't seem very comfortable in the truck."

He was right and so she went to change whilst he heated up the water, her need for comfort winning out over her instinct to argue back.

She changed into the oversized pyjamas that she usually wore for a night of gaming, and turned the corner from her bed just as he poured out hot water into mugs. "No coffee?" she teased, but took her mug happily, and let the heat warm her fingers through the ceramic. "Shall we sit on the couch?"

He nodded and let her lead the way. He didn't pull her close when she sat down, merely waited until she looked up at him over the rim of her mug and asked shyly if she could sit closer. *Then* he slipped an arm about her and pulled her in. They sat like that for a little while. She texted Abi to let her know what was happening, and got a smiley emoticon in return.

It should have been awkward.

Should have been weird.

But it wasn't. It felt right to be sat there, Marco's arm about her waist, sipping some hot water and just letting all of the stresses of that wild evening drift away.

When they'd finished their drinks, he got up and washed up both the mugs, before putting them to dry on the side. Then he turned and looked at her and she knew what he was going to say before the "principessa" left his lips.

"Do you have to go?" She really didn't want him to. She wanted him to stay more than almost anything, and she could see from his face that he wanted to stay too.

"Yes, principessa, I have to go. But I too have tomorrow off. Perhaps I could take you out for the day?"

Her eyes lit up and it was almost all she could do to stop herself from clapping her hands in excitement. "Really?"

"If you would still like to, that is. Maybe text me tomorrow and let me know? And I could pick you up around noon?"

"Noon sounds good." Bobbie walked him to the door, and swung her arms awkwardly before popping up onto her tiptoes to kiss his cheek. The look in his eyes as she did so made her blush, before realising, "Tomorrow I'll have had time to think about things clearly." She grinned at him cheekily, "So if I wanted to call you Daddy then…?"

"If you want to call me Daddy tomorrow, we can have a Daddy-principessa date."

Well, that was just fucking peachy.

※ 17 ※

When the sunlight streamed across her bed the next morning, the first thing that Bobbie did was reach for her phone. Marco had typed in his number the previous night, and she scrolled through her contacts until her finger hovered over his name.

She paused, and then put her phone down.

Coffee first.

Marco had been right the day before, no point rushing the decision. It was only eight in the morning; she had plenty of time to let him know that she was still up for their date. And if she was going to call him Daddy.

Once her coffee machine had dispensed some good old frothy caffeine, she sat on her window seat, sipping her drink, and having a think.

She knew other Littles, of course. One of their suppliers, Georgie, was an adorably sunshiny Little, and Lillie, whose workstation Bobbie had been working on the night before, had fallen in love with a reporter who'd come to do an article on Stuffie Hospital. And she'd heard both those Littles call their respective partners Daddy when they thought no one was listening. (It wasn't her fault people assumed that just because you were wearing headphones, you couldn't hear them talk at normal volume)

But did she really want to have a Daddy Dom of her own?

Bobbie wondered what Marco might be like as a Daddy Dom, and was immediately back in his arms, on the reception couch in Stuffie Hospital, being cuddled and petted and looked after. She couldn't remember the last time she cried in front of somebody. She didn't usually. Hated how people reacted when she got all overwhelmed: all pushy and telling her how to pull herself together and get over it. When she was overwhelmed, she couldn't get over it, she just needed to experience it.

If she was lucky, she'd manage to get herself out of the situation before the overwhelm hit, but if it did hit, there was no avoiding or 'getting over' the wall that smashed into her senses. It was pretty horrendous. Last night, thank goodness, had been an emotional overwhelm only, but that still meant that she'd cried in front of him. And he hadn't been pushy or mean, just kind and… and… *caring*. And she didn't know how she felt about that.

Just then, Kacie's name flashed up on her phone screen, and she answered immediately. "Hello?"

"Hey Bobbie, Abi told me about last night. Do you need me to organise the plumbing replacement this weekend, or just a clean up?"

"Clean up please; the emergency plumber is going to come back next week and do the assessment himself."

"Fab, I'll use our usual contractors. That work for you?"

Bobbie agreed, and then added, "Kacie?"

"Yes?"

"You know Turtle, the one you bought for me?"

"Yes?" This time the word was drawn out, like Kacie wasn't quite sure what was coming next.

"Why did you get him for me?"

"Because you needed him. You've always felt—" and here Kacie sounded a little apologetic, "—a little bit sad. But when you see one of the repaired stuffies, they really make you smile. So I thought…" her voice trailed off.

"I see. Do you think that's weird? That I'm weird, for wanting…well…stuffies. I'm a grown woman."

Kacie cleared her throat and Bobbie could almost see the other woman shifting in her seat. "I have a lion on my keychain Bobbie. Do you think I'm weird?"

"No, but…"

"And we all work with stuffies. Are Lillie and Ralphie and Rebecca weird?"

"No, of course not…"

"And Abi set up Stuffie Hospital. Is she weird?"

"No." Bobbie felt tears pricking at the back of her eyes and she blinked furiously, trying to keep them at bay. She picked up a cushion that sat on the window seat, and clutched it to her, clinging on to something for reassurance.

Kacie's voice was a little gentler now. "It's okay to go after the things that make us happy, Bobbie. Even if other people don't understand that."

How could that be the case though? Everyone knew that you had to fit in, or… or…

Or what?

Fitting in had never really mattered at Stuffie Hospital. Abi didn't care whether they came to work with pink hair or carrying a stuffie under one arm. She didn't care that Bobbie rarely spent any time with the rest of the staff, unless she absolutely had to, and she'd never minded Bobbie getting sassy and snappy when it felt like Abi was getting just a tad too close for comfort. She accepted them all, just as they were. She accepted Bobbie, just as she was.

"Bobbie?"

Oh shit, she'd been quiet for too long. "Yeah, fine. I suppose that's okay. The whole being happy thing."

"It is."

"Thank you, Kacie." She knew that the finance manager didn't like talking about this kind of stuff at work, and she could guess at what it had taken her to open up with her like this. "You deserve to be happy too, you know."

There was a bit of a stunned silence, before the two of them hurriedly ended the call before they shared anything else.

But after that, she picked up her phone and texted Marco.

Morning Daddy! What should I wear for our date?

❧ 18 ❧

Bobbie sat on the wall outside the townhouse, swinging her legs as she waited for Marco's truck to pull up. He'd been surprisingly cagey about where they were going, but had been pretty clear in his instructions as to what she should wear.

Comfy clothes and shoes today, *mia principessa.*

So, even though she'd wondered whether she wasn't being a proper princess by wearing a pretty pink dress, she'd done as he asked and had grabbed her comfiest pair of jeans, some trainers that looked like they had a rainbow racetrack printed across them, and a graphic t-shirt with the princess of another Italian plumber on it. She'd slung a leather jacket over the top, only briefly hesitating, before deciding just to be herself.

Yes, she was a Little, and yes, she was adorable, but she

would always be more nerd than pastel princess. This was who she was and he could take it or leave it.

By the look on Marco's face when he pulled up to the sidewalk, he'd take her.

"Mia principessa, you look so pretty!"

She rolled her eyes, but hadn't been able to hide how pleased his compliment made her, and soon she was strapped into the cab of the truck, next to him, and almost bouncing in her seat with excitement as she begged him to spoil the surprise.

"But I wanna know where we're going!!"

"You can wait."

"I don't think so," she sighed dramatically and threw herself back against the seat. "I might expire from all the tension, if I don't know where we're going soon."

"No."

"But *Daaaaaaaaaaddy*." She drew the word out before she even realised that she'd said it, but before she could freeze or panic, he leaned over to drop a kiss on her forehead, and then went back to waiting for the lights to turn green.

"Fine," and she sat and pretended to sulk, all the while secretly dancing inside at the fact that he hadn't gotten cross. He hadn't minded that she'd called him Daddy, or even that she was being a bit bratty. Instead, he'd *kissed her*.

She almost did a happy wriggle on the spot.

And she definitely did a happy wriggle when his truck pulled into the parking lot of the zoo. "*The zoo!*" This time she was so excited that her words came out all jumbled up. "We're going to the…Daddy Daddy Daddy…you're taking me to, are we really, oh my goodness, really really really Daddy?"

He was laughing so hard as he parked up, that he had to pause for a moment before pulling into the space. "You are so adorable, mia principessa. Yes, we're going to the zoo. Now, if you're really good, you can pick a stuffie to come home with you at the end as well."

That had her determining to be good, no matter how hard it might be. Because she was going to get the biggest stuffie she could find.

The whole afternoon was filled with treats. Daddy Marco had actually packed a picnic for the two of them, and he'd insisted that they started there, when he realised that she'd forgotten to have breakfast that morning. Sandwiches and little strawberries cut into the shape of hearts that she giggled over. And then an ice cream from the ice cream truck, before she slipped her hand into his and followed him round the rest of the park.

Her favourites were the otters who squeaked and bustled along, and even floated in their mini-river, holding hands, but the penguins were equally excellent, and she took a photo of a pair of sleepy lions to send to Kacie.

But possibly the best moment of the whole afternoon was when they came across a carousel in the centre of the park. Bobbie took one look at the queue of children with their parents and went to move away, but Daddy Marco refused to let go of her hand, and pulled her up to the kiosk, bought two tickets, and then helped her clamber atop a horse. As the music began and the carousel began to move, she threw her head back and laughed, joy bubbling over. Clinging on to the pole that held her horse in place, she leaned across and kissed him.

It was gentle and a little shy, a mere grazing of lips, before she sat back up and revelled in the glory of the carousel.

The delights of carousel had driven all thoughts of stuffies out of her head, until he took her into the shop, and she found a huge penguin stuffie with a tuft of hair on its head that reminded her of how his stuck up. And he'd bought it – his treat, he insisted – and carried it all the way across the parking lot until she put it behind her in the cab of the truck so it could cuddle her whilst Daddy Marco drove.

He came in to hers again that evening, and brought with him all the things to cook the most delicious mac and cheese she'd ever tasted. The way to her heart was almost certainly through her stomach, she thought, as she laid out blankets and cushions, so they could sit on the floor and eat it whilst watching cartoons. She'd picked ones with animals in – a nod to their outing to the zoo – and fell asleep curled up against him.

When she woke, the room was dimly lit by the warm glow of her lamp, and he'd pulled a blanket over them both.

"Hey Daddy," she whispered, as he'd fallen asleep too, and when he woke, blinking sleepily up at her, she didn't feel Little at all.

"Hey principessa," and that was all the words he said, but his eyes said so much more. And then he was sitting up, cupping her face in his hands and kissing her kissing her *kissing her* until her head spun and her lips were swollen from his kisses.

They pulled apart, breathing heavily, and she couldn't help but trace his lips with trembly fingers that longed to trace other parts of him.

"I would like—" her words were so breathy she barely recognised her own voice, "I would like to touch you, and for you to touch me and and and Marco will you make love to me?"

He stood then, offering her his hand, and pulled her up until she was flush against him. "Principessa, I would like that very much. Do you know what a safeword is?"

She nodded. "Traffic lights? Red, yellow and green?"

"Red, yellow and green work very well for me indeed."

Bobbie nodded and then tugged him towards the alcove where her bed lay. They tussled for a moment, discarding layers in a fervour that threatened to consume them both, until he picked her up and dropped her, naked onto the bed with a bounce.

She shrieked with laughter, and then reached out for him, pulling him down until his lips met hers once more and she was free to trace the lines of his shoulders, his belly, his thighs and then his hand was on hers, moving it until he paused, just before placing her hand on his hard cock. "Colore?"

"Green," she breathed. Lime green, emerald green, sage green, just green green green until everything that surrounded her was him. His cock in her hand, his mouth on her tits, his breath across her skin. She thought she'd lose herself in him, and hoped that she'd find her way out so she could lose herself over and over again.

His fingers danced their way down between her thighs, and kissed their touch along, up and then just *there*. She gasped and her sight whited out, the contact too much in the only good way that too much can be.

He kissed his way up to her neck and she gasped and cried out and begged him over and over for more.

"More, principessa?" he whispered, his breath hot against her ear. "You want more?"

She flung an arm out to her side dresser, rummaging around in the top drawer, feeling by touch for what she needed. Grasping it in her hand, Bobbie offered the condom up to him, meeting his eyes with a shy question of her own.

"Are you sure, principessa?"

"Please," she begged. "Please Daddy."

He groaned then and plundered her mouth as he tore open the packet and carefully rolled it down onto his cock. Then he shifted so he could lie next to her.

"I want you, my strong principessa. Come to Daddy."

Bobbie didn't need asking twice. She straddled him,

leaning forward so that she could tease his cock with her entrance, until he swore and told her to hurry up or he'd do it himself.

In that moment, something switched inside her, and Bobbie's eyes flashed a challenge at him. "I'd like to see you try."

She saw the moment Marco's eyes darkened, when a grin she hadn't seen before crept across his face, and he took her ponytail in his hand, wrapped it round his fist, and pulled until she fell against him, tits to chest.

"You want to test me?" The kiss he took from her this time left her breathless, and he nudged her hips into position. "You think I can't take *mia principessa* whenever I want?"

She moaned, low and desperate, and then challenged him again. "Try it."

His eyes searched for hers and watched as her lips whispered "green", and then he took her in one single stroke. She couldn't even move her head back to gasp because he still had one hand fisted in her hair, and the other arm holding her in place.

These strokes were hard, punishing, and she wanted more. More. *More.*

Words spilled from her mouth, unbidden, nonsensical as his cock hit her g-spot, and then her hair was loose, her head free as his hand went diving between her legs to press against her clit, like his cock pressed inside her.

Her head fell back and she was falling down down until a movement, a flicker of fingers, *something*, and she was shattering in his arms. Distantly, she was vaguely aware of his voice, hoarse and desperate in her ear and then he too was shattering.

Bobbie fell, loose-limbed, upon his chest, and he eased himself out of her, and rolled to dispose of the condom.

Then he moved her until she was on her side, and he could curl himself round her. "Mia principessa, you did so so well. Tesoro."

She'd lost all her words, he'd fucked them out of her, but she murmured contentedly, nestled against him, and fell asleep.

Bobbie woke up to the smell of something delicious emanating from her kitchen. Daddy Marco was humming? Singing? Whatever it was, it was vaguely out of tune and utterly charming.

She grabbed his shirt from where it had been tossed on the floor the previous night, and padded out into the kitchen. "Morning Daddy."

"Morning principessa." He leaned down to kiss her, a towel tucked round his waist, and an apron over the top to prevent splatter. "I had a shower and thought I'd make breakfast."

"Yum!" she said, and hopped atop a bar stool.

"Also, the pressure in your shower is not very good. I'll grab my tools and fix it later for you if you like."

"Breakfast *and* improved water pressure?" Bobbie giggled, "Sounds perfect, thank you."

She jumped down to get him some plates, and then cooed over what he'd made. Avocado on toast, with fried mushrooms and cherry tomatoes, and a smattering of grated parmesan. "It's better with pomegranate molasses," he apologised, "but I just made do with what you had in the fridge. I hope that was okay."

Considering half the food in Bobbie's fridge usually went off by the time she got round to cooking it, it definitely was. She was nicknamed the takeout queen by her neighbours for a reason.

"Thank you," she said, and tugged the top of the apron until he leaned in to kiss her again, a proper long good morning kiss instead of the original peck he'd given her. She took a bite and literally moaned. "This is *gooooooooood*."

Daddy laughed and swung himself onto the stool next to her. "My family like to cook. I like to cook."

"And I like to eat. Seriously, this is excellent. You may cook for me again." Bobbie pretty much inhaled the plate before being ushered into the shower whilst Daddy did the washing up. Again. She could get used to this.

"What're your plans for today then?" asked Daddy, after she'd gotten dressed in her favourite comfy jersey dress.

"Well, I think I'm going to swing by Stuffie Hospital, to make sure that all the clear up's going to plan."

He shot her a look. "I thought Abi said she was going to be doing that."

"Yeah, but I want to make sure it's being done properly."

He looked at her again. A proper Daddy look. "Abi said you should rest this weekend."

"Oh yeah," Bobbie found herself squaring off with him in what must be a fairly ridiculous sight. "Fucking my brains out last night wasn't exactly encouraging me to rest now, was it?" The moment she said it, she regretted it, because he looked less than impressed. "I mean…"

"I know what you mean, principessa. And I think perhaps someone has sat in her tower a little too long."

"Yeah, but…"

"Exactly."

"Exactly?"

"Your butt needs some discipline to help you behave. Excellent idea principessa."

Her eyes widened as she realised what he meant. "No! I don't want—" Her voice cut off as he took her hand and led her back over to the bed and sat down.

"Over my knee."

"No!"

"Principessa—"

"I won't!" Bobbie even stamped her foot a little. "You can't make me."

He stood up so suddenly that she took a few steps back, and then was running across the room, until he caught her about the waist. "Colore?" His breath against her ear was hot and her pulse thumped in her throat. "Bobby, what's your—"

"Green. Fuck you, it's green."

And then he hoisted her up in the air, as if she weighted nothing at all and was carrying her across the room and unceremoniously dumping her on the bed.

She crawled, as if to get away, but one hand held her firmly in place.

"Are you going to be able to keep still?"

"Are you going to be able to make me?"

One sharp slap to her ass took her breath away momentarily, and then he flipped her onto her back and held her hands together, up above her head. "I should tie you to the bed so you have to take your punishment."

The hitch in her breath gave away her desire.

"Oh principessa, you won't enjoy it nearly as much as you think."

"Wanna bet?" She was in full brat mode now and fuck was it glorious. To mouth off, to say fuck you, to break every rule in the damn book and to know that he'd still be there, he'd still stay. And that he loved it too. Pushing herself up, tussling with him, she freed one hand and used it to grab some rope from her drawer and throw it in his face. "Do your fucking best."

With deft hands he bound her wrists together, and then dragged her by them up to the top of the bed. Slipping an arm under her back, he rolled her onto her front, and then tied off the rope to the metal headboard. She kicked out behind her and he caught an ankle and tied it to the bottom post, and then the other, until she could barely struggle. He stood and watched her wriggling for a couple of minutes. She could feel his gaze searing into her back, and that only heated her more. Which made the cool rush of air against her ass even more shocking when he pulled up her jersey dress suddenly, and dealt a single smack.

"Uhh."

He chuckled at the sound she made, and ran his fingers gently across her cheeks, caressing, teasing until she was squirming beneath his touch, desperate to get away, but unable to do so.

Another smack, and this time she'd had enough. She wanted it. She needed it. And she was fucked if she was going to ask for it. So Bobbie opened her mouth and taunted him. "Awww…is that all you got Daddy?"

The barrage of smacks that peppered her arse after that particular witty retort must have lasted less than a minute, but already Bobbie could feel herself drifting into subspace, riding out the touch and the feel until she was almost floating out of her body.

"Colore?"

"Green, Daddy."

"Brava principessa, good princess," and then he started again. But this time he didn't let her catch her breath or settle into a rhythm; the strikes came in different places, at different times, on different beats, until she was gasping and then it happened. It happened again.

She cried in front of him.

And even as she cried, she wept the word "green" over and over, releasing everything she'd been holding. All the struggles, all the responsibility, all the strength that she'd had to have for decades, she let it all go and let her tears fall.

At some point, she wasn't sure when, he stopped spanking her. She was still saying green, over and over, but he was undoing her restraints and kissing her wrists and her ankles and her forehead, and pulling her into his lap so he could rock her back and forth.

"I'm so proud of you," she heard him say, when she was finally able to stop crying. "You did so well. Mia principessa. Mia bella principessa."

When she was able to sit up, hiccupping jagged breaths, he made her drink one glass of water, and then another, and then pulled her back down onto the bed with him, and told her to breath.

"It's okay principessa, Daddy's got you."

❧ 20 ❧

The next morning, Marco gave her a lift to work, wrapping his hand in her ponytail and pulling her down to give him a kiss in the car. It gave her such a rush that she'd almost skipped into the building, gaining odd looks from Warren, the stock manager.

"Are you okay there Bobbie?"

"Yes, thank you!" she'd beamed, and almost burst out laughing at the confused look on his face. Was she really always that reserved?

First stop was the Restoration Hub, which she was pleased to note was actually in far better shape than she'd left it on the Saturday night. She'd sidled up to Lillie, one of the restoration specialists and held out a rather sad looking Turtle in front of her. "I know you've probably got a backlog of clients, and I already rinsed him, but he's gone all flat and I don't quite know how to mend him."

Lillie gave her a searching, knowing look, and then took Turtle and placed him firmly on her workstation. "I'm ahead of schedule, so I can take today to work on Turtle and no—" she said sternly, the usually shy woman surprising Bobbie with her firmness, "—you can't pay anything. I know how important Turtle is to you, and it must be horrible not to have him in your toolbox."

Bobbie hadn't realised that anyone had noticed Turtle in her toolbox, and felt herself start to freeze up, but Lillie put a gentle hand out towards her and held it there. She didn't touch Bobbie, as if she knew, as if she had noticed, that Bobbie didn't really like to be touched. "I'd feel the same if something happened to my unicorn stuffie. It's okay, you didn't need to say anything or explain. I got you. He'll be ready to take home by the end of the day."

After that encounter, Bobbie needed some quiet, some space to herself, but when she walked into her office, she saw the mound of rescued stuffies, all crammed into her office. Exactly where she'd left them on Saturday.

She collapsed into her chair, the energy all draining out of her in one fell swoop. She didn't know where to start. Where could they go? There was no point moving them back into the Restoration Hub until Daddy – *Marco*, she corrected herself, *he has to be Marco when I'm at work* – had checked the rest of the pipes. But this many stuffies, this many stuffies without homes, without people? It was more than she thought that her heart could take.

There was a clearing of a throat, and she swivelled in her chair to see Abi at the door to her office. She tried a light-hearted "Hey Abi," but the look her boss shot her indicated that she wasn't fooling anyone.

"Come up to my office?"

"Fuck, yes please."

Abi's office was painted in warm colours, and when they both entered, Bobbie felt her shoulders relax a little.

"Your weekend went okay? With Marco?"

"Oh yes, that was great." Bobbie fought the blissed out look she knew would decorate her face if she wasn't careful.

She failed. "It was *really* great. But don't worry, we'll be able to work together professionally. That won't be a problem."

"Then what is?"

Bobbie sat down on the floor cushions that scattered one corner of the office. She'd never done that before. Most Stuffie Hospital team sat on the floor cushions when they were having one to ones with Abi, she said that they made everyone feel a little more equal. Bobbie had always wondered what was wrong with a chair. Well, what was wrong with a chair at the office, because now she was thinking about picking up floor cushions for her apartment and having a gaming marathon with Daddy sat on them.

Abi sat on a cushion next to her and waited.

"I love working here. I always have done, because I can just be me. Or at least, I *thought* I could just be me. Only this weekend makes me wonder if I have been being me." Once she started talking, she couldn't stop. "We've known each other what, fifteen years? You co-signed my mortgage. You know more about me than anyone in the world, and yet I don't think I've ever had you round for dinner."

"I co-signed the mortgage," said Abi gently, because you worked hard to save that money, and because I have known you for fifteen years, I knew you weren't going to screw me. I didn't do it for dinner."

"No, but I *should* have cooked you dinner. What do I think? That I'm going to have someone over for dinner and then I'll somehow lose myself? That they'll start running my life?"

"There is a power imbalance at play here; I'm older than you, I co-signed your mortgage, I'm your boss."

"Yes, but you did that because you're a decent human being. And what did I do? I work hard at work, sure, but I don't know anyone at work. Not properly." Her words were out of control now, and Bobbie found herself close to tears for the third time in four days. "I've fucked it all up. I was trying so hard to keep it all together, that I forgot how to live." She took a deep juddery breath, and then let it go. "Fuck. I need to go to therapy."

"I can recommend an excellent practice," said Abi with a laugh. "And if you want to have me over for dinner – *want to*, mind you, not feel like you should – then I would love that."

Bobbie looked at her. "Sure. I'll order takeout. I don't think that subjecting you to my cooking would aid this whole getting to know each other thing very well. I'm not sure you'd make it dessert." When she laughed this time, it felt like a huge weight had been lifted from her shoulders. That hadn't been so bad. She'd spilled her guts and yes, it had been a little embarrassing, and also a little rambly, but it hadn't been too bad.

She shivered.

That was enough sentiment for the time being.

"Okay, so where are all these stuffies going to fuck off to, because they can't all live in my office forever."

$\begin{array}{ccc} \text{❧} & 2\,\text{I} & \text{❧} \end{array}$

At lunchtime, she'd stumbled into the staffroom, looking around a little wildly at a space that she only really entered to do some jobs. Lillie and Ralphie, the patchwork specialist, looked up in surprise when she sat down at their table, and plonked the mystery sandwiches that Daddy had wrapped up for her in front of her.

"So, what brings you to our humble table?" asked Ralphie in a chipper, singsong voice.

"Sandwiches?" she muttered, but she shot an awkward smile at him in an attempt to be friendly.

"Finally!" he announced, Lillie rolling her eyes next to him, "The mystery of our stoic site manager is to be revealed. Tell us, oh silent one, what's in your sandwiches?"

"I don't really know," she admitted, and then added, "my maybe boyfriend made them for me?"

That comment had resulted in a torrent of questions (primarily from Ralphie) and a few interjections (also from Ralphie) and when lunch was over, Bobbie left feeling ever so slightly shellshocked, and when the patchwork specialist came and knocked on her office door an hour later, she braced herself.

"It was really nice to talk to you today," he said. "I know I'm loud, and people say that I'm a lot, so I hope I wasn't too much."

"No," said Bobbie, and realised that she actually meant it. "I'm not really used to chatting to people much during the work day, or at all, really, and I'm trying to change that. You were really easy to talk to, and I felt super included. Thank you for that."

He smiled then, a shy thing that felt far more genuine than all the bright laughter he'd shared with her at lunch, and she felt a rush of warmth towards him.

"Hey Ralphie?"

"Yes?"

Taking a deep breath, Bobbie said, "I need some help. I can't find anywhere to put all these stuffies from the Great Wall, and they can't stay here, it's too depressing. And they can't go in reception, because they're so sad looking, they'll put off potential clients."

"I've an idea," he said immediately. "I'll be right back."

And by the time Marco came to pick Bobbie up from her office, after he'd finished doing his assessment of the pipes, she was laughing and joking with Ralphie, whilst Nate Pace, one of the stuffie designers from upstairs was ordered back and forth, carting stuffies from her office to his. She wasn't entirely certain how Ralphie had managed to persuade him, but she wasn't going to complain.

When she saw Marco she bounced over instinctively, before stuttering to a halt, inches from his lips.

Other people were around, but when she glanced over her shoulder, Ralphie was too busy piling stuffie after stuffie on top of a clearly long-suffering Nate to pay any attention to her. And besides, did it really matter? She went on tiptoes and kissed his cheek. "Hey."

"Hey principessa, how was your day?" He dropped a kiss on the tip of her nose and she giggled.

"Good, thank you." And then, emboldened by all the hands of friendship she'd offered that day, added, "Well, it was actually pretty tough. I'm trying to make more friends at work, and it's a bit scary." She dropped her head and fiddled with the edge of her t-shirt.

"Ah, I'm proud of you, mia cara. That sounds like a really good idea."

Bobbie nodded enthusiastically. "I think so. And I'm going to get a therapist as well. I need to talk about my things."

His eyebrows drew together, and she realised that her Daddy was worried about her. "Because of yesterday?"

She rolled her eyes at him. "Like you don't know that yesterday was awesome."

That furrow between his brows lessened, "I just wanted to check, principessa. It's always important to check."

"Fine, I'll allow a check in." The cheek in her voice had him looking a certain kind of way, and she squirmed beneath his gaze.

"Someone is trying to change the subject."

That brought her back down to earth with a thump, and she nodded slowly. "That's fair. We're still getting to know each other, and it's not something I'd really like to talk about at work, but if you're not busy this evening...?"

"I'm not busy this evening."

"Then maybe I can talk to you about some of it then. Maybe."

"I'd like that principessa. I want to make sure that I can always look after you the way you need to be cared for. And I can only do that if I have all the relevant information."

"Are you guys going home to fuck?" Ralphie's voice cut in without a moment's warning.

"Ralphie!" Nate looked horrified. "You can't ask that!"

"Sure I can," said Ralphie, completely unrepentant. "Bobbie's my friend now, so I can ask that. And," he added, his voice suddenly serious, "I can check that she's being looked after, too. Bobbie needs someone to look after her. She spends far too much time being responsible."

"I quite agree," said Daddy Marco, and Bobbie fought the urge to brat them both.

"I'm quite capable of looking after myself, you know."

"We know," said Ralphie, "but you shouldn't have to do it all the time." He looked at her closely, and then grinned a grin that she could only describe as sparkling. "You just need a Daddy to put you in your place, and then to spoil you rotten."

Her face heated, and she almost buried it against her Daddy, pausing only because it'd prove what Ralphie said as true.

"Enough," said Nate, and this time Ralphie did look a little repentant. "That is not okay, Ralphie. You can't say things like that without checking that they're okay with it first."

Ralphie nudged Bobbie, who was looking stalwartly at the floor. "I'm sorry Bobbie, it's just that he keeps calling you princess, and I've seen—" he stopped and looked at Daddy Marco. "I didn't mean to—"

She felt, rather than saw, her Daddy reach out and place a hand on Ralphie's shoulder. "I know Ralphie, you just got overly excited. One of these days, you're going to cause a Daddy a whole lot of trouble." And Bobbie could have sworn that she heard Nate mumble "Ain't that the truth" under his breath. "But mia principessa is still a little shy. She'll talk to you about things on her own timescale, I'm sure."

But when they were in his truck, driving back to hers, he

spoke pretty seriously. "Principessa, Bobbie, I need to tell you something."

Her heart dropped and she felt a bit sick, because those words, in that particular configuration, never boded well. "Do you have to? Is it bad?"

"No no, it's not bad, but it is important that you know. I said I'd had Little ones call me Daddy before?"

She nodded.

"Well, that's partly how I know Ralphie. Not—" he added hastily, "—that I've ever dated Ralphie. But I was seeing a Little boy, a friend of Ralphie's, before he moved away. And that means that Ralphie, and a number of people in town, know that I like being a Daddy."

He went to continue, and she held up her hand to pause his words. "One minute please."

It wasn't that she needed a moment over him having been a Daddy to other Littles – that she didn't mind – but she needed a moment to process that other people knew that. That other people might guess, if they saw her with him, that she was a Little too.

That was a whole lot.

She was only just opening up to the idea that she should try and open up to people enough to make some friends. Have someone other than Turtle or Marco inside her apartment, and now she was giving people an automatic insight into something so very private about her?

Her hands shook, and she rummaged through her bag until she found Turtle. Daddy Marco was quiet, just kept driving, but she saw that he looked sad and as much as she wanted to ease his worry, she couldn't. She just couldn't.

"I don't care about your exes," she said at last, her words shaky, "I have exes too; we've had lives before we met. It's the other thing. The fact that people *know*." Turtle was softer than he'd been in years, now that Lillie had finished his repairs, but Bobbie was going to wear out a patch of his fur pretty damn quick if she wasn't careful. "People can't know that about me. Most people barely tolerate me as it is. They'll call me a freak, a weirdo, a—"

"Stop." The word was quiet but a silencing effect. He pulled up outside the townhouse and put the car into park. "Bobbie. You are not a freak, or a weirdo. Everyone around you knows that. You seem to be the only one who doesn't."

Silent tears fell down her cheeks, but this time it wasn't because of everything else, it was because of him. Her Daddy was disappointed in her, she could tell. It had been too good to be true; of course they ended up here, with him frustrated with her lack of confidence, her inability to tell the world to go fuck itself when it really mattered.

"I understand. I'm sorry. I'll go."

But he took her hand when she went to open the truck door, and looked at her in confusion. "Cara mia, you're not hearing me. No one could possibly think that about you. And if they do, then they are not worthy of having such a beautiful principessa grace their life. Now, I'm not going to tell you that everything will change, because it won't. But I do think that getting a therapist, like you said earlier, is an excellent idea. And until such a time as you can believe it for yourself, I shall remind you that you are precious and special and my beautiful girl, just as you are."

She choked back a sob, and he leaned forward and kissed her softly.

"Beautiful Little one, mia principessa, I've got you."

"Daddy! I can't find the sauce!" Bobbie called across her apartment to where Daddy Marco stood chatting to Abi, balancing a tray of nuggies in one hand, and searching the fridge with her other.

It was her first time hosting a party for her work colleagues, or at least, the ones she felt comfortable enough to have in her flat, and that meant nuggies and chips and the most basic of basic buffets. Dips, finger food, even chopped up vegetables after Daddy had made noises about there needing to be at least *some* vegetables. She'd prepped it all herself, had managed not to burn the nuggies to a cinder, and was pretty impressed with the spread she'd laid out.

Besides, her Little friends were fully on board with the finger food, Ralphie and Lillie sitting on the floor with bowls, and Nate and Abi had seemed to take it in their stride. Kacie had looked awkward and hovered, as if she didn't quite know where she should sit, but she'd come. And Bobbie recognised what a big deal it was for Kacie, because it would have been a big deal for her too. Kacie needed lots of love, she thought, and then all thoughts of friends flew out of her head as she almost upended the tray.

Daddy Marco rescued it from disaster, deftly setting it down on the breakfast bar, and pulled out a bowl of homemade ketchup for her from the fridge. Made with real tomatoes and everything. He'd reluctantly agreed to ketchup in her fridge but only, he'd insisted, if he could make it for her. She'd never tell him, of course, but it definitely tasted better than the bottled stuff. Just one of the perks of living with her Daddy. Homemade good, daily packed lunches, and the best water pressure in the city. She was a very lucky girl.

He spun her round and gave her a quick peck on her nose. "Excellent job, cara mia. There may well be a treat for a good principessa this evening, once everyone has gone."

Treats were all very well, but Bobbie was already wondering if she could taunt him into spanking her – because that was punishment and treat all rolled up in one.

"We'll see. Maybe I'll have a treat for you, Daddy." She grinned mischievously up at him, and suddenly felt so utterly happy. This was her life, with her friends and her Daddy. It couldn't possibly be any better.

"I'm sure you will," and he pulled her close, tweaking her ponytail, and running his fingers across the back of her jacket. "I love you Little one."

"I love you too Daddy." And she kissed him.